Pink Sky at Night

Pink Sky at
Night

CAROLINE CRANE

DOUBLEDAY & COMPANY, INC.
GARDEN CITY, NEW YORK

LIBRARY OF CONGRESS CATALOG CARD NUMBER 63–12882

To
Muriel Fuller,
with gratitude
and affection

Pink Sky at Night

Chapter One

Her finger looked bare without the ring. Bare, and a little humiliated. There was a tiny mark all the way around where the ring had been.

Gillian closed her hand into a fist. That was a childish trick, pretending it was the finger that mattered when, at nineteen, her whole life had been smashed.

For a year she and Betty Hartledge had ridden the Sunday evening bus back to junior college. Betty had asked so many questions about Jim, had seemed so interested. So kind, Gillie had thought. So lovely to want to talk about what was closest to Gillie's heart.

But three weeks ago—just three weeks ago today— Jim had told her it was over. Gillie could not believe it. They had loved each other. But after a while she had remembered to give him back his ring, and now Betty was the one who wore it.

Gillie's father pointed out that if the young man was going to be flighty, it was good to find it out before she married him.

With a start, she realized where she was. She had been drawn, in her aimless, brooding walk, to the little house Jim had bought for her. It was a darling house, set back from the road and part way down a bank so that it appeared buried in trees and flowers. It was an old house, too, with steep stairs, thick walls, and a pump outside that was no longer used. She stood on the other side of the road looking at the house, the early June sun falling hotly on her shoulders.

Betty was to be a July bride.

At the sound of a car approaching behind her she began to walk quickly away. The car slowed.

"Can I give you a lift, ma'am?" said a man's voice.

Gillie was relieved that it was only Ward, her brother. It didn't matter if he saw her standing heartbroken by the house.

"Isn't ma'am for married women?" Gillie asked as she climbed in beside him.

"Not necessarily."

Ward's round, placid face, now glistening from the warmth of the day, showed a look of irritation. Gillie knew she was boring her family with her shattered love, but how could she talk of anything else when there was nothing else that mattered to her? Certainly they must understand that.

He took out a handkerchief and mopped his flushed face. Ward was too beefy to stand the summer heat. He took after their mother, who was small and plump, while Gillie resembled their tall and rangy father, "Bone" Polk. It was only fifteen-year-old Jean who had gotten the best from everyone—Dad's slimness, Mom's more moderate stature, and, from a grandmother, blond hair besides. Jean was pretty and smart, and no one would ever treat her the way Gillie had been treated by Jim.

"I've been showing another farmhouse," said Ward. "Everybody wants to retire to farmhouses. Drop you off home? I'm headed back to town."

She nodded. How clever he was to stay clear of entanglements and heartaches. At twenty-eight he was still a bachelor. He had a house of his own on a pretty street in Mistra where he lived his stuffy, comfortable life and ran his real estate business.

"What were you doing over there by the cottage?" Ward asked.

"How did you know where I was?"

"It figures."

"Then you can probably figure out why I was there."

"Yeah, but what for?"

He braked the car suddenly to avoid a rabbit that dashed cross the road. Annoyed with the rabbit, and seemingly also with Gillie, he continued, "You won't get him back by moping."

"I don't want him back," Gillie said. "I only wanted to see the house again. I couldn't help it. It was supposed to be my house, and—and it's still part of me."

"Why don't you cut out the drama? I thought you gave up drama with your last play at college."

Memories came rushing back, memories of only a few weeks ago. She had been so happy acting in the play—so happy graduating and being engaged—until she had found out on the night of the play that Jim would not be coming to see her perform. It should have been a clue. He had promised, and his excuse was flimsy. If he had cared he would have come, and to her graduation, too, which he had also missed. She had been too stupid to see that he was lost to her. She had seen nothing until he had told her outright that he no longer wanted her. He had had to *tell* her. And all the while, Betty had known.

"If it weren't for Jim, I wouldn't have given up acting," Gillie told her brother.

"What do you mean you wouldn't have given it up? You can't act in school plays when you're not in school, and what else is there?"

She clasped her arms tightly across her stomach and shivered a little.

"There's the whole world," she said.

"Huh?"

They turned onto a smaller road that sloped down into their father's farm. Ward stopped the car and turned abruptly to face her.

"There's the whole world," Gillie repeated. "And I want it."

"You feeling all right?"

"I feel better than I have since—Ward, I think I

know what I'm going to do with myself. You'd laugh, but it's something I've wanted all my life and I never told anybody. I only gave up thinking about it when—when I thought I was getting married."

Gillie leaped from the car and ran toward the house.

"Oh, boy," said Ward, shaking his head. He backed around and left.

She banged through the kitchen door. "Mom? Mom, where are you?"

The house was empty and she rushed to her room, the only downstairs bedroom in the house. Dotted Swiss curtains framed the windows that looked out on an apple orchard.

"Room, I'm leaving you," Gillie told it.

The curtains fluttered as though in response. Gillie looked about at all the things that were so familiar to her. Already they seemed a part of the past. She felt excited and impatient.

Maybe this was supposed to happen. Maybe marriage to Jim had been the wrong fork in the road after all, and the dream she had sometimes dreamed secretly was really supposed to come true.

The hurt flooded back and again she was confused. How could Jim have been wrong for her? He had been the reason for her whole existence. But whether it was right or wrong, it was not to be. Betty had seen to that, and now the other fork would be the one she would follow, if she could.

She jerked open the drawer of the writing table and took out her bankbook. She had worked hard in the summers, and part time at college. The results were there—a little less than five hundred dollars.

I can do it, she thought. I have to. I have to get away from Mistra, from Jim. I have to be somebody again.

Gillie sugared the berries for a pie, mixed the crust, and cut up vegetables for stew. No doubt her mother was wondering at this sudden helpfulness. They had all been so indulgent with her in the last weeks, and she, Gillie saw now, had done little but feel sorry for herself.

"Mom," she began, "what would you say about me going to New York?"

"I think it would be a nice holiday for you, dear."

"I mean, to live. Mom—" her voice came urgently, desperately. "I can't stay here. I have to get away before the wedding. I mean—I have to. There's something I want to do in New York. At least I've got to give myself a chance. I think that's the only way I can really forget."

She waited for her mother to ask what it was.

"I knew you had fun last summer," said Mrs. Polk. "Is that it? You're thinking of going on and acting some more?"

Gillie swallowed. She felt her face beginning to warm.

"How did you know? I never told anyone."

"It was written all over you like a book that summer the Mistra Playhouse opened. You were thirteen and we all went to see it, remember? I thought you'd never stop mooning. Then you went all out for television and movies—"

"It wasn't only television and movies," Gillie said. "Remember how I scrimped every year to go to the Playhouse in the summers? That was my real love. It was so wonderful I could hardly stand it. I almost forgot to worry about being too skinny and gawky for an actress, and I—"

"Why, you're a *nice*-looking girl."

"Oh, Mom, please. Anyway, that didn't stop me. And every time I got a chance to act at school, I loved it. Then last summer when I got the job at the Playhouse I thought I'd burst. It didn't matter that I was only painting scenery and making coffee."

"What do you mean only? You got a chance to act."

"Yes," breathed Gillie. "Twice. I didn't have any lines, but I was there on the stage. It's the most magic feeling in the world."

Gillie wondered. Was it really more magic than love?

"Then," she added, "I gave it all up for Jim."

Her mother frowned. "It sounds pretty wild to me. My daughter an actress. And living in New York by herself."

Gillie stared, wordless with shock and disappointment. Her mother saw the look.

"I'll have to see what your father says," promised Mrs. Polk.

That evening after dinner, Gillie and her parents sat in the living room to discuss it further. Jean stayed nearby reading a book.

Gillie looked at her sister, musing: She'll be doing this herself one day. *She'd* never even consider getting stuck here in Mistra, not with her brains. Why did I have to be such an idiot? I should have planned on flying off to New York the minute I finished college.

But she *had* planned on it, Gillie realized, until she had fallen in love with Jim.

"Where would you stay?" asked her mother. "You don't know a soul in New York."

"In a hotel?" Gillie quavered.

"Your money wouldn't last a week in a hotel. Not a proper hotel."

"You'll stay in one of those hotels for women," Mr. Polk said sternly.

Her mother looked as though she might cry. "My poor little girl, you're only nineteen."

"Goodness, Mom, kids younger than I am go abroad by themselves. Ward was only eighteen when—"

"He was in the Army, dear."

"Yes, but—"

16

"You'll stay in one of those hotels for women," her father repeated. "Someplace that has a nice chaperone."

Gillie knew she would have to act sensibly if she were ever to get her way.

"Maybe the vocational counselor at college would have a list of places." She kept her voice low and mature. "I'll phone them tomorrow."

The discussion was over for the time being. She went to her room and turned on the light. A breeze moved the curtains, and outside the window the apple trees stood quietly. What would the city be like?

She rested her face on the screen. Fireflies rose slowly like sparks from the grass. Up on the highway the lights of a single car passed by.

Gillie felt choked with sadness. She was leaving home. She was headed for the Naked City, the Asphalt Jungle, where you could be hopelessly lost and lonely among eight million people, because nobody cared what happened to anybody else. You could, she had heard, die on the street and no one would pick you up because they would think you were drunk.

But there were theaters and television studios. There was glamour and glitter and the chance to be somebody—or at least the chance to have an interesting life.

She was to have been Mrs. James Albert, and to have lived Jim's life along with him forever and ever. She flung herself away from the window and buried her face in the bedspread. Forcing her mind back to the city, she tried to imagine acting there. She had often been on the stage at high school and college. Twice, for a whole week each time, she had been onstage at the Mistra Playhouse. She remembered how it was—the odd, confined little world in a lake of light and, out beyond, where the fourth wall was missing, the blackness and the people. When you couldn't see them, they seemed to number in the thousands.

Would Broadway be the same? If all went well, she would know.

She rose and stood before the mirror to comb her hair. She made herself smile. Someday soon, that face—glamorized, of course—would be in all the county papers as the Mistra girl who had gotten a part on Broadway. Then it would appear again and again as she went on up the ladder to greater and more magnificent things, and her family, instead of doubting, would be proud of her.

Chapter Two

Gillie's first glimpse of New York startled her. Eerie gray giants reared up in the distance beyond the north New Jersey flatlands—the skyline of the city. Pressing her bangs against the window, she whispered: "New York."

The people in the bus were restless. Many of them had been traveling most of the day, and it was Sunday, too. Gillie wondered how she would get her luggage down from the rack without killing somebody. The poor old apple-green bags were growing worn, not surprisingly, after two years of college. But her initials were still on them in faded gold—G.P.—for Gillian Polk. The more she said the name over to herself, the worse it sounded. Perhaps she could change it for the stage. No, she argued, for then it would not be herself, but someone else who was achieving *her* fame and success.

The bus moved more and more slowly as the traffic around it thickened. The road seemed to swirl down into a canyon, and after a while all the wheel sounds together became a hum inside a tunnel that passed under the Hudson River.

The Port Authority Bus Terminal was tremendous. It teemed with bewildering crowds such as she had never seen before. She stood for a while, marveling. Then, lugging her bags, she went in search of a taxi stand.

"Eighty-third Street, please. Three twelve and a half."

"East or West?" said the driver, staring ahead through the windshield.

Gillie fumbled in her purse for the address. "West, I guess."

"You sure?"

"It says W. Eighty-third."

The taxi wound its way onto a highway that ran above the street beside the pier-lined river. On the other side of her was the city. Gillie did not know which way to look. The driver said nothing, explained nothing. How could a person grow so used to all this, she wondered.

This is my home, Gillie thought as she stepped from the taxi to face a row of brownstone houses on a quiet, pleasant street. Where was the shining skyscraper she had imagined? She climbed the steps of three twelve and a half and walked through double doors into a dim and fusty parlor.

Girls passed through the hall and a few glanced at her curiously. Mrs. Ingram, owner of the residence club, came out of the office to greet her.

"We're so happy you can be one of us," she said to Gillie. "Did you have a nice trip? How did you come, by plane?"

They sat down on a sofa and Mrs. Ingram told her about the club.

"You know when breakfast and dinner are served, of course. And here's your room key. Now then, we want our girls to try and be in by midnight, but if for some reason you're going to be out later than that, stop at the desk before you go and ask for a key to the outside door."

Under the rain of instructions, Gillie's mind paused to remember her father's concern for proper chaperonage. She would write him about these rules. It should make him very happy.

Mrs. Ingram's gaze moved past Gillie. "Oh, Dulce, there you are. This is your new roommate, Gillian Polk."

A dark-eyed girl about her own age, wearing shorts and an expensive-looking shirt, stood in the parlor doorway.

The girl smiled. "Dulce Rodgers. Hi." She took one of Gillie's suitcases and led her up three flights of stairs.

"Ghastly climb," said Dulce, "but it keeps you trim. Well . . ." She pushed open a door. "Here's home."

The room faced south and was cheerfully sunny. The walls were gray, the floor was green linoleum, and the bedspreads were a noncommittal white.

Gillie walked over to the open window. Below her were concrete courts, back walls, and small gardens. Street noises and the shouts of children came up through the window. Girls screeched in the hallway, and someplace nearby a bathtub was running.

"Enchanting, isn't it?" Dulce said deprecatingly.

But Gillie, gazing out the window, thought it really was enchanting.

"Did you come here to study?" Dulce asked.

"No, I want to get into acting, if I can."

"Well, good luck to you. You'll need it."

I can try, can't I? Gillie wanted to say.

She must have looked hurt, for Dulce added, "It's a great, big rat race, that's all I know. But heck, you might be the one who'll land on top. I'll be plugging for you. Wouldn't it be fun if you got famous?"

"It would," said Gillie. "More than fun."

She turned to unpack her suitcase and, as she did so, caught sight of herself in the mirror above one of the dressers. Her hair was blown about and her face was shiny and tired. What a mess. What a world away from the girl she tried to imagine herself to be. But somehow she would become that girl and somehow she would act.

She looked again at her unfortunate reflection. Would she make it? Oh, would she?

After a while, Dulce changed into a skirt and they went downstairs to dinner. For the first time, Gillie saw the girls she was to live with. Thirty or forty

strangers sat at rows of tables jammed into an under-
sized room. With a sick feeling, she thought of home.
They were probably eating dinner there, too, and
they would be thinking of her. They would be wondering whether she would make her way in New
York, or whether she would come home defeated
when her money ran out.

An exquisitely fragile blonde, sitting opposite,
handed her a glass of iced tea.

"Florence, meet my roommate, Gillie Polk," said
Dulce. "Florence Hale, Gillie. She's in the professional class at the School of American Ballet. Waiting to be discovered."

"They know I'm there," said Florence with a laugh.
"I'm waiting for someone to care."

Gillie watched her graceful hands. How beautiful
she was! And a professional ballerina. There were
several dancers in the building, Dulce had said, and
singers, too. It was going to be fun, living among
such people.

When dinner was over, the two roommates walked
along their block to Riverside Park. Except for its
rocky hills, it was exactly as Gillie had pictured a
city park—children and dogs, a playground, and an
ice-cream man.

They strolled down a path toward the river.
Small boys fished over a wire fence. On the bank
behind them, couples lolled in the grass and more
sedate people sat on benches watching an excursion
boat go by.

"I thought the city would be all hustle and bustle," Gillie remarked. "This might be Mistra with a river running through it."

"This is where people come to recover from the hustle and bustle," Dulce told her. "Would you rather we went to a movie?"

"Oh, no, I like it here."

The last time she had gone to a movie it had been with Jim. She closed her eyes. *Jim.*

"What's the matter?" Dulce asked.

"Nothing. Just tired, I guess."

She decided not to talk about Jim. The mark on her finger was gone now and no one in New York, her new home, ever needed to know of her defeat.

"If you're tired, maybe we ought to turn in early," Dulce said. "I have to get up for work tomorrow anyhow. Hope I don't bother you."

"Don't worry about waking me early. I'm a farm girl, remember? Besides," Gillie added, "I want to get up, too, and start my career."

Chapter Three

West Forty-fifth was only a narrow, soot-tinged street, busy with trucks and taxis. Was she disappointed?

No, thought Gillie. How could I be?

A giant photograph of two famous faces looked out from the wall beside her. Above her head the marquee shouted their names and the name of the play. Down the length of the block there were other marquees, other theater entrances. She was here at last. This was where she belonged.

Florence Hale, who had danced for a while in a musical, had given her some tips. There would not be much casting for new shows now, at the beginning of the summer, Florence had said. But replacements were always needed, especially for long-run hits. She advised Gillie to keep her eyes and ears open.

Gillie realized with dismay that she had not thought to ask how or where to begin her search.

Past the next theater she saw an alley leading back from the street. At the end of it—the stage door.

It was an unassuming old door, but she knew it at once. She knocked and waited. Passers-by could see her from the sidewalk. They would wonder what she was doing, knocking on a stage door. Of course that was not the way to go about it, but what was? Here, at least, she might learn. She knocked again. The door was opened by a squat old man in a shabby suit who peered at her with scorn.

Gillie stammered, "I was wondering—I'm new here and I don't know what I should do to get a part in a show."

"You one of them actress kids?" snapped the man. "What's this, some new angle, coming around here? Whaddaya think you're going to find? I ain't no producer, lady. I just work here. You want to audition, go see the producer. Don't come to me. I ain't no producer, I can't give you a job. You go tell your agent he sent you to the wrong place. . . ."

She backed away and was hurrying toward the street when she heard him call, "Hey, lady." She turned. "Show's closing for the summer anyhows. Try again August-September. But don't go coming to me."

Don't worry, you won't be seeing *me* again. . . . Gillie fled, longing for the courage to shout something back at him.

What a miserable day it was. A dog day. The steamy sun left no protection, even in the shade. She felt sticky and covered with grit. A drugstore, deliciously air-conditioned, beckoned at the corner of Broadway. She sat for a while at the counter, sipping a Coke.

On an impulse, she slid into a booth and phoned Dulce's office. A woman's voice answered, "North American Television."

"What?" said Gillie.

"North American Television. Hello."

She controlled herself enough to give the extension number. "Why didn't you tell me?" she cried when Dulce answered. "You work for one of the biggest TV networks, and you didn't tell me."

"Gil, old girl! Are you calling from home?"

"No, I'm somewhere near Times Square, and I— Oh, Dulce, I don't know anything! What do I *do?* I just had this awful little man making fun of me and I thought he'd never stop, but nobody gives me any help."

"Why don't you come over for lunch? I can't stay on the phone too long. You can walk here, it isn't far."

Soon Gillie stood within the immenseness that was Radio City's central building. This was what she had expected of New York. This, and not Ingram House. It was a world in itself. She went to a desk marked Guided Tours and asked for the NATV offices.

Dulce met her in the company's reception room. "I won't take you back where I work. You'd be disillusioned."

"That's what you think," Gillie said. "I've never seen such a palace."

"It's only a front. Inside, where they keep us working girls, there's paint peeling off the wall. Now, how
about Schrafft's?"

The restaurant was almost as crowded as the bus
terminal had been the day before. They had to wait
in line for a table. Dulce explained that it was always
so at lunch places in the business district.

When they were seated, Gillie told her about the
morning. She found her adventure at the stage door
less embarrassing now. In a bitter way, it was almost
funny.

"What I'd like to know," she concluded, "is where
you find these producers."

"Oh, they have offices around. But there must be
some other way. Know what you should do? When
we leave here, go back to Broadway or Seventh Avenue, stop at any newsstand, and get a paper called
Performers Only. They always tell who's casting."

"*Performers Only*," Gillie breathed. She put her
hand to her mouth. "Dulce, what a nut I am. I
heard the actors at the Playhouse talking about it,
and now when I need it, I forget completely."

"Well, after all, it's your first day."

Pensively, Gillie stirred her iced coffee. How confident she had felt about coming to the city! Never
could she have imagined what a big, busy, and
impersonal place it was.

"Speaking of forgetting," she said, "how come you
didn't tell me you work for NATV? Here I am, come
to New York to be an actress—"

Dulce shook her head. "It's not going to do you any good. I'm in the advertising end." She buttered a roll. "And I don't know anybody important. Only the kids I work with."

"What's the advertising end?"

"Sponsor contracts."

"Well . . . that's my kind of luck. Anyhow, thanks for reminding me about *Performers Only*. I guess I don't seem very ready for all this, do I?"

"I don't know, I think you've got as much as anybody. Maybe more, because you're an individual and not a copy, like a lot of kids. You've got good looks for the stage."

"Me? Do you mean me?"

"Who do you think I mean?"

"Me, with my mouth too big and my ski-jump nose?"

"Stop running yourself down," said Dulce. "You have very cute looks. Your nose isn't ski-jump, it just turns up a little. And you wouldn't want a tiny mouth. Tiny features don't show up on the stage. You could do something with your hair, though. Why don't you let me work on it?"

When they left the restaurant, Gillie walked in the direction her friend pointed out until she found a newsstand that carried the paper. After glancing over the headlines—items about the Straw Hat Circuit, which meant summer stock—she searched for a bus that would take her back uptown.

Buses roared past her, all going in the wrong direction. The sidewalk was jammed with people, rushing and pushing. Gillie looked in the store windows as she went. What an insane place Broadway was. Blaring record shops, dazzling movie houses, junky little stores that sold practical joke kits and fake shrunken heads. It was horrible and fascinating, but not what she had expected. The Broadway Gillie had imagined was a sedate avenue of theaters and brilliant neon signs.

Her feet were aching, and still there were no buses. Just ahead of her, some people were getting out of a taxi. Gillie slid into it and closed the door, trying to keep from thinking of the extravagance.

"West Eighty-third Street," she sighed. "Three twelve and a half."

Ingram House was quiet in the afternoon, for most of the girls were at work. Wearily, Gillie changed into her bathrobe and lay on the bed to read *Performers Only*. Movies, TV, variety acts—and news of the summer theaters that had opened in June. She felt a tightening in her stomach. In a few days June would be over, and early in July, Betty and Jim would be married.

She turned the page. There was a call for night-club dancers. An off-Broadway show needed eight Negro singers in their thirties. There was nothing for Gillie. Nothing. And in a little while Betty and Jim—

Her eye fell on a photographer's ad—his prices, his list of famous clients. She sat up, studying it.

The next instant she was out in the hall where a classified directory hung on a string beside the coin telephone. *Theatrical Managers & Producers* filled two and a half columns. She would send each one of them her picture and résumé. After that, every week or so, she would call to remind them of Gillian Polk. They would have no chance to forget her. In self-defense they would be forced to see her.

"Whoop-pee!" She flung the paper into the air. Snatching up the page with the photographer's telephone number on it, she called to make an appointment.

Chapter Four

Gillie had gone to a hairdresser the day before and slept with her head wrapped tightly in a turban. It was hot, but worth it. The hair-do she had worn since ninth grade was gone. The shoulder-length wave was cut short and the side bangs brushed back into a swirl.

"My forehead's too high for this," Gillie had cried.

"You'll get used to it," the hairdresser answered.

When she looked at herself in the morning, she was pleased. It wasn't Gillie, but why go on being the old Gillie when this was such an improvement?

She packed a bag with the clothes Dulce had lent her. Both of them had shaken their heads over Gillie's wardrobe. It was so small townish and unsophisticated. As soon as she had a job, she would throw out everything and buy clothes that befitted a chic young actress.

A creaking elevator in a very old building carried her upward to *Borisov, Theatrical Photographs.* She arrived at the studio half an hour early to allow time for getting ready.

Mr. Borisov had another client when she came in, a bleached blonde in tap shoes and leopard-spotted leotard. Between shots he handed Gillie a stick of greasepaint. It would photograph best, he said. She opened the stick. It was dark orange.

A make-up table, its mirror bordered with lights, stretched the length of the dressing room. Along the opposite wall was a rack of tawdry costumes. She sat at the table, studied her face in the merciless lights, and began daubing on the paint. She darkened her eyebrows and outlined her eyes. With a brush, she traced on her lipstick.

When he had finished with the blonde, Mr. Borisov came back to her.

"Here, you want some costume? You get eight pictures, eight changes wardrobe." He shuffled through his rack of wilted finery.

"I brought a few things," Gillie said. "A couple of blouses and a formal. I thought I'd do two pictures in each outfit. You see, I want something I can use for television and the stage."

He nodded. "I thought maybe you a showgirl." He jerked his head toward the blonde, who was leaving. Gillie wanted to stare, but Mr. Borisov took her face in his hand and turned it toward the light.

"Where is your eye make-up? This little bit is no good under lights."

She returned to the dressing table and penciled

33

her brows until they appeared grotesque. Layer after layer of mascara gave the illusion of false eyelashes.

Looking about the bare little stall, she remembered the names in the photographer's ad and thought of all the celebrities who had probably changed their clothes right in this same room.

I'm one step closer, she told herself. At least I'm in a theatrical place and I'm doing something about it.

She did not have long to daydream. Mr. Borisov was calling her before the camera.

He planted her among what seemed to Gillie a thousand lights, and turned them all on. Her anticipation changed to fidgets as he carefully adjusted each lamp and moved them about to achieve the best effect. Then he took his place behind the camera.

"Bend back," he ordered. "No, no, only a little. Turn the head a lit-tle bit left, no not so. No, a little more." He strode from the camera to set her in position. "Bring the right arm front."

It was grueling. She tried to fix her mind on the glittering future, but she felt like a plastic mannikin, pushed and pulled in every direction.

"*Smile!*" said the photographer.

She smiled.

"No, no, is no good. You scare everybody. You must mean it."

She was stiff and nervous. Gradually he made her feel freer before the camera lens. He knew what she should do to dramatize her type and her individuality. With his own brand of sputtering patience he coached her in each pose.

He took two ingenue shots of Gillie in the dress she had worn to the studio. For the next two, she swathed herself in Dulce's black woolen cape. Under the hot lights the wool was prickly and made her feel faint. Mr. Borisov posed her, first so that she was laughing wickedly, and then screaming.

"For producer of detective program," he declared.

Finally, in the strapless formal that seemed to make her bones sharper than ever, Gillie portrayed a charming hostess. Borisov handed her a make-believe cocktail of solid plastic from his large supply of props. She raised the glass and, feeling awkward and childish, toasted the camera. Then her session was over.

"Girls, girls, girls," said Dulce in the dining room that evening. "I'm sick of girls."

"It's an awful lot like a dormitory," Gillie agreed.

"*Like* a dormitory! It *is* a dormitory. They even give you dormitory cooking. The only edible part is the iced tea." Dulce poured herself a glass and gulped it down. "I wonder what the beverage is in winter."

"Weren't you here in winter?"

"No, I came last month. It feels like ten years already. I tried living at home, out in Harrison, and commuting, but it was awful. Be thankful you're not an only child, Gil. At least your parents have other kids to concentrate on."

"Where's Harrison?"

"Out in Westchester. It's just another suburb."

"Is this your first time living away from home?" Gillie asked.

"Hardly. When I was a kid, they sent me off to boarding school. Then I went to college for a year. Didn't study, so I flunked all my subjects. What a break!"

"What, flunking?"

"Mmm. I was such a dunce they kicked me out, so off I went to Europe. I stayed a whole year. It was divine." Dulce stared at the plate that was set before her. "Good grief, what's this?"

Gillie prodded her own with a fork. "It looks like hash and sweet potatoes."

"They can't be serious." Dulce nibbled at the limp salad, drenched in vinegar. "Guess what. I got picked up today."

"Picked up! By a man?"

"Well, anyway, it was sort of a pick-up. I met this—oh, you'd adore him." She squeezed Gillie's arm. "He's an actor. I was having lunch in a drugstore on Sixth Avenue and this boy was sitting next to me, so we started talking. Of course I told him about you."

"What's he in?"

"Oh, honey, just because he's an actor doesn't mean he's *in* anything. Actors are usually between jobs. But he's been on television a few times and he's done a couple of off-Broadway things. He's going to try to get tickets for a show Friday night. I've never been out with an actor before. Won't that be mad? He is sort of mad, but in a nice way."

Gillie wondered at her carefree roommate. She was the type of person who, without ever making an effort, got through life with the minimum of bumps. How did they do it? Of course money helped, and Dulce came from a wealthy family. Those beautiful clothes, which had impressed Gillie on their first meeting, were never bought with a typist's salary.

"Daddy's in advertising," Dulce had explained the day before. "Mother's a clubwoman. It's so darned typical. You get the feeling they live that way just because they're expected to. But then, I suppose, what else would they do?"

Dulce lit a cigarette. "How was your sitting?" she asked.

"Great. Wait till you see the pictures. If I'm the least bit photogenic, they ought to be good. He actually made me relax."

"You can do wonders once you get those pix. I looked at your paper last night and saw a lot of calls for TV commercials. Why don't you try that?"

"*Commercials?*"

"Look, dear, are you an established actress?"

"Well, hardly."

"Then who are you to be so choosy? You'll never

make it if you don't start by getting yourself noticed any way you can."

TV commercials, Gillie pondered. How she despised them! Probably Dulce did not share her feelings, for the advertising end was Dulce's business. But how could Gillie—Gillian Polk, who wanted to be a serious actress—how could she make herself turn handsprings over a scouring powder, or sing paeans to a deodorant?

A voice at her shoulder whispered, "Gil, it was only a suggestion. Come on, let's get away from these ten thousand clacking females. Let's go out to the park."

Chapter Five

There was hardly a sound that Saturday morning as most of the girls slept. Gillie had the bathroom all to herself. She took her time making up in welcome peace.

When she returned to the room, Dulce was awake. "How come?" Gillie exclaimed. "You were out till all hours."

"I know. Isn't it mad? After the show we went to a coffee house in Greenwich Village, and there were these people playing guitars. Not entertainers, just kids. It was wild. We *sang*, Gillie! Folk songs! They're so informal down in the Village. You'll have to go sometime. I wish I lived there."

"How was your actor?"

Dulce kicked her legs into the air. "*Mon acteur! Mon acteur!*"

"Do you really like him? You seem awfully *très gai.*"

"Sure I like him, but it's nothing serious. Just fun for both of us, for a while."

"How can you tell?"

"Because that's the way I planned it. Everything. Basically I intend to go out with respectable young men who are all good prospects. But just to make life worth living, I've got to have a few loonies. Then I can give them up with great regret, along with my youth, when I marry someone who can support me."

Gillie bit her lip. How orderly it sounded. But what would happen if Dulce's feelings ran away with her? Or perhaps she could manage that, too.

"What's his name?" Gillie asked.

With a sound like the cooing of a pigeon, Dulce cuddled her face into the pillow. "Bar-ney," she sighed contentedly.

After eating breakfast by herself in the almost-empty dining room, Gillie started out. An hour later she was in Mr. Borisov's studio, seeing her pictures. She studied each of them again and again. Remarkably, they were not bad at all. A little stiff, perhaps, but only the hostess pose was pretty near impossible.

"Now what do I do?" she asked the photographer. "I've got to take these around to leave with producers, and—"

"But you cannot. These are proofs. You have to have composite."

"Oh, I know that, Mr. Borisov." What did he think she was? "Uh—" She twitched her foot in embarrassment. "Exactly what is a composite?"

"Here is composite." He reached into his desk. Out came an eight-by-ten sheet made up of four different shots of the same actor. "You put the name, the telephone number on back, your description, age, experience—" He shrugged. "Then producer know if they want you. How many you want? 'Bout feefty?"

"I want five hundred," Gillie said desperately.

"You better to start with feefty." He named her a price and together they selected the four best poses.

Another long wait loomed ahead. He told her he would have them by Wednesday. She was paying for all these days in New York and her progress was at a standstill. Things would have to happen, once she got her composites.

Aimlessly she wandered toward Times Square. What would she do all afternoon? She had to be doing something. For some reason, she knew that she had to be busy.

Then she remembered why. *This was the day.* How could she have forgotten? How could she have waked up and seen the sunshine, talked to Dulce, eaten breakfast, taken the bus to Mr. Borisov's—and not remembered?

It was Saturday. The weekly Mistra *Citizen* came out on Thursdays. She would have to wait until, perhaps, a week from today, and then when she saw her mother's handwriting on an envelope, she would know what was inside. She would open it and there would be the clipping. One more of those familiar stories she had always looked at with sentimental interest because they were girls she knew. And there would be the photograph of the bride—the bride who should have been Gillie.

An advertising sign on a billboard over Times Square was flashing, alternately, the time and the temperature. Eleven-thirty, it said. It was still morning, and they were being married in the afternoon. Dizzily a scene flashed before her. The phone would ring at Ingram House. There would be a call for her, or a telegram. Jim would have changed his mind.

No, it would not happen. He would never change his mind again, and Betty would not let him. The thought of it made Gillie churn inside. Would she even want it to happen? Of course not. It was over, it was done. Jim had left her.

But if, by some wild chance, he should—then she would have him back. She would have her cosy cottage and her life all planned for her. To her alarm, she felt a sob coming. She was being stupid. That cottage and that life were Betty's now. This was no fairy tale. Gillie was through with those people and with Mistra. She had gone beyond them into a bigger, shinier world.

Her heart was full of feelings that tossed and tore at each other. She took a breath and tried to clear them all away. She had the whole afternoon. If she spent it at Ingram House doing nothing, she would probably lose her mind.

Her eyes traveled down the row of movie theaters

until she found a feature she wanted to see. The admission was high, but today she deserved it. Here, amid the cool air and the celluloid distractions, she would spend Jim's wedding day.

Chapter Six

Wednesday came, but Mr. Borisov did not have her composites ready. He had been out for several days with a cold and all his work had piled up. He was finishing the priority jobs now. She was to call him on Monday.

She left the studio—helpless. Without her pictures she could do nothing.

The new edition of *Performers Only* was on the newsstands. She bought a copy and sat on a bench in Duffy Square to read it. An old man next to her dropped some pieces of potato chip, bringing flocks of pigeons cooing and flapping about them both.

Suddenly Gillie held her breath. An audition notice! It was for an off-Broadway show—something small and unimportant. But as Dulce had said, she would never even get a toe in the door if she were too fussy right now in the beginning. She held her paper stiffly, for a moment staring blindly at the pigeons while she made up her mind. Then she crossed the street to look for a telephone booth.

They would see her that afternoon. It was a private

audition and she would not have to read in front of a crowd of experienced actors.

Supposing I did have to? she wondered. I think I'd die.

Gillie took a bus to the east side of town. The audition was being held in an old brick church. She was met by the director of the group, who led her to the cellar where there was a low platform stage and rows of rickety chairs. He told her the story of the play and left her with a copy of the script to look over. She read through the speech he had pointed out, trying to say it aloud to herself. While waiting for him to return, she glanced about the room. She had expected Broadway when she came to New York—a theater like those on West Forty-fifth Street. What had happened to her? This was all a bad dream. It had to be. The Mistra Playhouse was more exciting than this.

"Okay, how about it?" said the director as he reappeared. "Have you done anything like this before?"

"You mean, Greek chorus?" Gillie asked. "Well—not exactly."

"Try reading me that bit I showed you."

The play was *Hippolytus*. It was the first time she had ever heard of it. She frowned at the page and began.

"O would I were nestled in some hidden cave, there to be turned by the hand of Zeus into a bird amid the winged flocks! I would rise and soar to Adriatic's wave-dashed shore and to the waters of Eridanus. Into that glooming tide the sorrowing daughters of the Sun, in their grief for Phaëthon, weep tears of amber brilliance."

She stumbled, wondering whether to read it as verse or prose. What was she supposed to be feeling? He had told her the story, but what had these lines to do with it? She faltered over the names and the director had to help her.

Somehow she finished the speech and was given another. At last he took the script from her.

"I'll be in touch with you," he told her. "Do I have your name and where to reach you?"

On Saturday, as she had predicted, there was a letter from Mistra waiting in her mailbox. Gillie knew exactly what was in it. She took the letter up to her room, where she would be alone for a while. Dulce had gotten up too late for the Ingram House breakfast and was eating out at a drugstore.

First, the note from Mom. It was a chatty letter, not saying much. What could you say about a week with the Polk family?

She reached for the clipping. Almost before it was unfolded, a vise tightened around her heart. The photograph was exactly as she had imagined it—the round, doll-like face, the generous dark curls, the lacy veil.

It had been held, of course, in the town's most

fashionable church, which Betty did not usually attend. She had had four attendants and a reception at the local golf club. It was the big day in Betty's life. She was the star for that one day, playing her part for all it was worth. Afterward her glory would fade away until she was a housewife like anybody else.

"Well, look at you. Heat prostration?" Dulce stood in the doorway.

"I guess so," Gillie answered as casually as she could. "We don't have this kind of humidity in Mistra."

"The worst part is, you'll never get used to it. Guess what I had for breakfast, Gil. A banana split! I was walking out to Broadway and all of a sudden it hit me— I'm free! I can do anything I like and there's no one around to care. Of course I wouldn't eat that way every day, but isn't it fun to know you can?"

Gillie dropped the clipping into her stationery box. She practiced smiling to herself for an instant and then she turned to her roommate.

"You're out of your mind, Dulce Rodgers. Next time you do a thing like that, tell me so I can go, too."

It was the kind of fun Betty would never know.

I wonder if that director ever will call, Gillie thought as she lay in bed.

It was almost a week. Maybe next week. More likely, never. "Don't call us, we'll call you," was so familiar it was a show business joke. She had learned that from the actors at the Playhouse.

What would happen when all her money was gone? That time was not so very far away.

"Dulce, what's going to happen to me if I can't get a job?" she asked softly. Dulce gave a little moan and rolled over.

Gillie got out of bed and took two aspirins to help her sleep.

A whole extra week had been lost, but by Wednesday, at last, her composites were ready. This might be the turning point. Anything could happen! She dressed as smartly as she could, made up carefully, and left for the studio. The résumés, which she had typed on a machine borrowed from one of the girls, were in her hand.

Of course she had known the price beforehand but, opening her purse, she could not help a feeling of panic. It was more than a week's board and room. She handed the bills to Mr. Borisov and watched while he wrote out a receipt. He let her sit at his desk to fasten her résumé sheets onto the backs of the composites.

She left with the bundle in an envelope under her arm. With it, she could almost reach out and touch the future. Her whole career was contained in these pictures.

Dulce had been right about one thing. Nearly all of the calls in *Performers Only* were for television commercials. At least they would provide an income until she found a part in a play. And she would be seen. Perhaps even discovered.

Several blocks away and nine floors up was the first office. She stood in the corridor trying to muster the self-assurance she would need from now on.

They want *me*, she told herself. They want new talent and I'm it.

It gave her the courage to go in. "I noticed your ad for actresses—" she began.

With a practiced smile the receptionist cut her short. "Do you have pictures?"

"Yes, I have." Gillie's voice was mellow and carrying, her best. She reached into the envelope and produced a composite.

"Thank you. I'll be sure that Mr. Rossman sees it." Gillie hesitated.

The girl said, "We'll give you a call if we have anything for you."

Gillie left the office. It had taken about a minute. Was that all there was to it?

"To what?" she muttered furiously. "Just what did you accomplish, Miss Polk?"

Try as she might, each one of her visits went the same way. There was never anyone but the receptionist in sight. It would be a wonder, she thought, if all the Mr. Somebodies actually did see her picture. And a positive miracle if anybody called her.

She stood on the sidewalk in a quandary, the hubbub of Times Square going on around her. A slick-looking man with a leer asked her if she was lost, baby. Abruptly conscious of her heavy eye make-up, she darted across the street to a drugstore. At the counter no one would bother her.

She started to order a soda—but no. No more money must be spent. She felt the unpleasantness of staring eyes as she huddled by the paperback stand to go over her list. The only remaining entry was a television serial asking for twin boys and an elderly woman.

That took care of *Performers Only*. The next edition would not be out for a week.

She fled the drugstore. The people there were hateful—happy and complacent. Vegetables. They wanted nothing great out of life. And for all that, they could afford sodas when they were miserable.

She began to run almost blindly toward Broadway. There was one last dollar in her purse, for a taxi home, so she could hide in her room and cry. But a taxi was not for her. Not when she would have to go on making the rounds—who could guess how long? She could be sure that none of those invisible men or their ice-cold secretaries would call her.

Reaching Broadway, she turned northward and kept on. She had all the time in the world and not an extra cent of money. Instead of taking the subway home, she would walk. It was thirty blocks.

Chapter Seven

The buzzer rang four times—her ring. Who could be calling at ten in the evening? Gillie flew downstairs.

"No phone," said Dulce, meeting her at the foot. "That was me buzzing. I wanted you to meet Barney."

"Why didn't you tell me?" whispered Gillie. "I'd have combed my hair."

"Barney won't mind. He's not pretentious." Dulce led her into the sitting room and presented Barney Lazar.

He was not at all the dark and moody actor Gillie had pictured. He had red hair, a cheerful grin, and an air of insistent individualism.

"How about some friendly advice for my room-mate?" said Dulce after they had talked awhile. "You've been in the acting game a couple of years."

Barney answered with a smirk. "The friendliest advice I can think of," he said, "is forget it."

Dulce jabbed him with her elbow.

"No, seriously," he continued. "You're not Equity, are you?"

"Actors' Equity? The union?" Gillie was ashamed at how little she knew about it. "Even when I was in summer stock I didn't get into Equity, because I wasn't being paid. Besides, I was mostly an odd-job girl."

"Too bad. Stock's a good way to get in, sometimes." Barney seemed relieved that he had an excuse to offer for her lack of success. "You'd have it a whole lot easier if you were Equity. A lot of auditions are only for Equity people."

"You mean," said Gillie, "it's harder to get a part if you're not a member? But how do you get a part so you can become a member?"

"Sort of a dead end, isn't it?" he agreed. "But there are a few non-Equity productions now and then, off-Broadway. They won't get you your membership, though."

"I might as well give up," said Gillie. "I can't even get a reading for a part. I've been to almost every producer's office I could find, and I've yet to meet a producer. I'm sick of those people at the front desks. All they do is thank me for leaving my pictures. Some of them won't even accept my pictures. What do I do now?"

"Now you start all over again," said Barney. "You keep going back and reminding them you're available. Someday you'll show up someplace just when they're looking for a girl your type."

"You mean *that's* the way you do it? Just *chance?*"

"I'm glad I don't want to act," Dulce put in.

52

Barney smiled, as though recalling his own first days. "Not all of it," he told Gillie. "You hear about auditions and you hear who's casting. Actors have quite a grapevine. Stick around in actors' hangouts, drugstores in the show business area. Join an acting class. You get a lot of info there."

"I can't afford it until I have a job," Gillie said.

"Well, you're on the right track. Keep trying. Get around, get yourself known. You signed up with any registry?"

She shook her head.

"It's a good idea," he said. "They take all your calls so you don't miss any while you're out making the rounds. Sometimes they hear about casting, too, and they have tie lines to some of the networks. Try the Wynn Registry. That's the one I use. I've got two roommates, but nobody sits home and answers the phone."

"That's like an answering service," Gillie said. "Isn't it expensive?"

"No, it's not the same thing. It's just an office with a switchboard. You put that down as your number, so all your calls go there instead of your home. It'll cost you five bucks a month."

"Five a month?"

"Listen, everybody uses a registry," he urged. "It's worth it, believe me. Otherwise you lose a lot of calls. They've got a lounge, too. You can rest while you're making the rounds. Take your shoes off."

He scribbled the registry's address on a note pad from his pocket and handed it to her.

"How can I lose a lot of calls when I don't *get* a lot of calls?" Gillie asked.

"You sound as if you need cheering up," said Barney. "How about it, you free on Saturday? My roommates and I are having some people in. Very informal. Dulce'll be there and we thought you'd get a kick out of meeting a few more savages."

It would be her first bit of social life since coming to the city, Gillie realized as she went upstairs. How lucky it was that Dulce had found Barney. This was going to be fun, and it might help a great deal, knowing other actors.

The Wynn Registry was full of people—aloof and sophisticated show people. But the lounge was pleasant and, best of all, air-conditioned. It would be worth the money just to have this place to come to during the day.

She went to the desk and registered, leaving with them a composite in case they heard of any jobs. I have an *in*, she thought, sitting down on one of the sofas.

After a while, as Barney had suggested, she slid off her shoes. She opened *Performers Only* and relaxed.

At nine o'clock on Saturday evening, a time when parties in Mistra were usually well under way, Gillie and Dulce left Ingram House and took the subway to Times Square. Leaving the safety of the crowds behind them, they walked through slums and darkened streets toward the river.

At first Gillie was sure the building must be deserted. There was one bare bulb above the door, which only heightened its desolate appearance.

Dulce opened the door to a sour smell of cats and old cooking. "Boy, we're adventuring." She hunted for the bell. "Lazar-Kane-Costa. That's them."

"Are you sure this isn't a joke?" Gillie asked. She stopped, amazed to hear the answering buzzer. There was actually life in this house.

They went inside, and Dulce giggled. "It is sort of scary, isn't it? I bet it's a hangout for a dope ring. We're only a couple of blocks from the waterfront, and—"

"Dulce, stop it."

They climbed a flight of stairs so off balance that Gillie felt certain she would be pitched over backward at any moment. On the fourth and top story, Barney stood in the hallway with a quart of club soda and an opener in his hand. He grinned. Out of pure relief, Gillie smiled back.

Barney introduced his two roommates, Hovis Kane and Ralph Costa, and the half dozen others in the room. They were a motley crowd of off-beats who showed little interest in the newcomers.

Gillie looked about curiously. There was hardly any furniture in this dilapidated apartment. Yet a feeling of intimacy came from a single light bulb, painted red, and several candles perched in empty chianti bottles.

A tubby girl with short dark curls seized the soda from Barney's hand. "This is ridiculous!" she cried in a deep voice. "Let's throw it all together and make punch. Got anything to mix it in?"

Ralph Costa produced a plastic dishpan and they poured in their soft drinks with ice cubes and lemons. The girl, whom the others called Marsha, stirred it with a large wooden spoon. Scooping up a paper cupful, she held it out. "Who wants?"

Barney took the drink and tasted it. "Put sugar in."

With a whoop, Marsha added sugar. While she and Ralph worked over the drink, Dulce began to make friends.

Gillie sat on the floor in a breeze from the open window. She felt out of place and lost. At home she had always known practically everyone, and then she had had Jim.

"Can I offer you some of this poison?" said a Texas accent. Hovis Kane was giving her a paper cup. As she took it, he sat down next to her.

"It isn't that we're all on the wagon," he explained. "It's just that the better brews are out of our class."

"That's fine with me," said Gillie. She tasted it. "Not bad at all."

"They were lucky this time."

He asked her about herself, and listened with knowing sympathy as she told him of her stay in New

York. He was an actor, too. The three of them—
Barney, Ralph, and himself—were all in the business.

"I haven't had a break yet," Gillie said.

"You shouldn't have come in the summer," Hovis
told her. "You should have done stock. There's
hardly anything going on here now. We've been at
stock before, but we decided this time we'd stick
around. Barney had a TV date, and Ralph and I
were in a show down in the Village."

They talked more of acting. "Now take that girl
there, Marsha Greenfield," he said. "She more or less
fell into acting and she's doing all right, too."

"What do you mean, fell?"

"She's an artist. See those oils on the wall? They
had her doing the design for some off-Broadway
show, and being around the business, she kinda slid
right into acting."

"Have any of you," Gillie asked, "been on Broadway?"

"Na-a-aw. Broadway!" Hovis looked disgusted.
"The pay's okay, but the shows aren't much. Ah suppose," he added, "if anybody offered me a part, Ah'd
take it." With that, he got up and left her.

Gillie continued to sit alone. She edged toward
Dulce, who was chatting with a tall, good-looking
Negro boy. He was talking of a concert he would
soon be giving.

"What do you play?" Gillie asked.

He looked at her with amazement. "I don't play, I
dance."

"Modern dance," Dulce added eagerly.

Gillie retreated to the window. Would she ever be anything but an amateur? All these people were *in* something. They were rehearsing and performing while she was only hoping, and even her hopes were growing tattered.

"How are you doing?" Ralph Costa knelt beside her.

"Oh, I'm fine. Your floor's so comfortable I don't feel like moving," she apologized lamely.

"That's the nicest thing anybody's said about our floor." He found a bowl of pretzels and set it between them.

Ralph looked more like a truck driver than an actor. He was dark and muscular, though not very tall. His eyes, as he talked, glowed with an earnest intensity, and his broad, strong face was sensitive and expressive.

He did not stay with her long, for soon he was up and busy with Marsha again. Gillie drank more punch, ate pretzels, and studied Marsha's paintings on the wall.

All of a sudden she found herself being squeezed farther back toward the window. They were starting a game. Gillie looked about in surprise. Wasn't this group much too sophisticated? She supposed they were, in many ways, but they were childlike, too.

It was a guessing game. One person stood in the middle of the room and, by asking three questions, tried to discover the identity of another person chosen by the group. Hovis was the first to do the guessing. At every one of the three questions, Marsha would boom in her monstrous voice, "You're so *right!*" or "You're so *wrong!*" The rest of the time she filled the air with raucous laughter and loud, jovial comments. She purposely prolonged her own turn at guessing, relishing the center of the room and all attention on her.

"Come on, Marsha, get off the stage," said one of the boys. "Here's a little girl who hasn't had a chance."

Gillie felt her face go pale. What was the matter with her? She wanted to perform and this was almost the same, but these people made her nervous. They were successful while she was not.

I want Jim, she thought. If Jim were here, and still in love with me, I'd be the life of the party. I'd be better than Marsha, even.

She rose. They were all looking at her. She had said she wanted to be an actress, and they would not understand if she refused. After endless minutes of incorrect guessing, she was removed from the floor. Ralph was smiling at her. He was the person she was supposed to have guessed.

"Anybody know Indications?" cried Marsha. "It used to be so fashionable."

They divided into teams for Indications. Gillie was relieved that it was to be a team game, but her relief did not last long. They were writing on slips of paper the names of songs, poems, books, movies, and the catch phrases of advertising slogans. Each slip would be given to a member of the opposite team, who would have to act out his title or slogan in pantomime clearly enough for his teammates to guess what it was. The titles were chosen for their impossibility to perform.

Dulce was the first, and her slogan was "It's the money that makes the difference." Gillie could not help laughing, though she knew the choice had been accidental.

Then came her own turn. She opened her paper. "Always," it said. She stared at it dumbly. How in the world could you act out "Always?"

The time for planning her act had passed. She looked at the group. "I don't know how to do this."

"You gotta!" bellowed Marsha.

She knew the tune of the song, but not the words. During her summer at the Mistra Playhouse she had minded the record player for *Blithe Spirit*. "Always" was the music used when the maid was put into a trance. She closed her eyes, trying to remember the scene. The maid had worn a bandage. Gillie tied a handkerchief around her head and pantomimed it as best she could. Her team was stumped.

"Do it again, please?" someone said.

At that moment Ralph looked up. "*Blithe Spirit?*" Astounded, Gillie shook her head.

"One word?" he asked, and guessed the song. They slapped him on the back. Still bewildered by his success, he joined the team in congratulating Gillie on her performance.

Marsha had been given "In Flanders Fields." Magnificently she died in battle and lay with her arms forming a cross over her head.

It isn't fair, thought Gillie. That was an easy one. I could have done it myself.

But she could not have done it with Marsha's brilliance. She did not have the dynamism. She noticed that Ralph, who had praised her for her own skit, had now turned back, full of delighted admiration, to Marsha.

It's only a game, Gillie told herself. Who cares about a silly game?

Chapter Eight

Gillie was aware of Dulce scrambling about, dressing, and tiptoeing from the room. Was she going to church? Probably not, in Bermuda shorts. Then Gillie fell asleep again.

"Hey, Gil! Gil!"

Sun was pouring in the window and it must have been late. She had missed breakfast! There was a little money left. After being such a failure at the party last night, she deserved some consolation. She would go out to the drugstore for a banana split.

"Gil, are you focused?" Dulce stood at the foot of Gillie's bed, holding a disarranged Sunday *Times*.

"What're you doing up?" Gillie asked foggily.

"I can never sleep after a late night out. I'll feel it tomorrow, but now I'm in great shape. This is the first time I've gotten up for Sunday breakfast since I've been here, and I went out and bought a paper—"

"So I see."

"But, Gil. Look!" Dulce flung open the paper and rapped it wildly with her finger. Gillie's sleepy eyes could barely see the print. "It's made for us!" Dulce cried.

Gillie squinted at the page and saw what it was. "You're out of your mind. We—we live here."

"Who," demanded Dulce, "would live here if there was any way out? This is made for us, I tell you. Two and a half rooms, kitchenette, a hundred and fifty a month. And it's furnished."

"*A hundred and fifty?*"

"Figure it, Gil. That's seventy-five each. Ever so much less than we're paying now. And we could have our own telephone, and cook all our meals in our own kitchenette and never have to eat this slop again. It says August first occupancy. Oh, come on, Gil. Say yes. Apartments go fast in this city. I'm sure it's been snatched already, but if it hasn't—Gillie, say yes, and I'll throw on a skirt and run over there. It's only four blocks. Gillie. *Gillie?*"

Already Dulce was changing into a dress. Gillie could not think. What a wild thing to be confronted with on waking up in the morning. She tried to follow Dulce's accounting. With the cost of groceries, it still could not come to more than she was paying at Ingram. But there was something so binding about having an apartment.

"Don't you want to see it, too?" Dulce asked.

"In my pajamas?"

"I could make them reserve it, and then you come over as fast as you can."

She was gone, without remembering to give Gillie the address.

There was nothing Gillie could do but go out to Broadway for her banana split, and then come back and wait. She was in the sitting room reading an abandoned comic paper when Dulce returned, her face red with excitement.

"I hope you don't mind, Gil. There were some other people there—they couldn't make up their minds and the super was getting impatient. I knew if I waited they'd probably take it, so I grabbed. I had to pay a month's rent in advance and another for deposit, but we get the deposit back when we move out."

Numbly, Gillie calculated. All of a sudden, in a single morning, she owed Dulce a hundred and fifty dollars.

"They gave me the keys," Dulce went on. "Why don't you come over and have a look, right now? It's cute! It faces back, like our room here, so we won't get street noise. They'll be painting it during the week and we can move in on Saturday."

Still unbelieving, Gillie followed her to Eighty-seventh Street. The building was a well-kept brownstone with a red door.

"We're apartment 3B," said Dulce. "One less flight to climb."

The living room was small and cluttered, but pleasantly bright. Dulce apologized for the furnishings. "We can cover the couch and armchair. But the

nice thing about the couch is, it's a sofa-bed, in case
we want to have a house guest."

Gillie began to feel superior to the girls still stuck
at Ingram House. Now she and Dulce were truly independent. There would not even be a Mrs. Ingram
to fuss about hours and noise. They would be
bachelor girls living in a New York apartment, and
that was supposed to be wonderful fun.

Dulce opened two broad doors at one end of the
living room. "Forgot to tell you. *This* is a kitchenette.
I didn't really know."

It was all in a neat row: the sink, stove, refrigerator, cupboard. The kitchen was not a room, but an
alcove, actually part of the living room.

"It has its advantages," Dulce said. "You don't have
to leave your guests while you're fixing dinner."

Gillie explored further. There was a windowless
bathroom with a pink tile bath. There were two
clothes closets. The bedroom was so small that the
twin beds and the one large bureau left scarcely any
floor space.

"I don't like their curtains," she muttered.

"No, their decorating's a crime, but we can change
that easily enough."

Gillie curled up in the single armchair. She was
tired. Was it weariness from the party last night, or
was it discouragement? Slipcovers, curtains, a hundred and fifty dollars . . . Her share of the groceries,
and incidentals such as cleaning supplies . . . She
would have another week's rent to pay at Ingram

House, too. Her mind groped to remember her bank balance. When it came to her, she subtracted the new expenses.

"Dulce—" Her voice was drained. "I don't have enough to pay you back."

"That's okay. You can owe me."

"You sound awfully cheerful. Do you think I'm a good risk?"

"Oh, sure. You'll turn up something pretty soon."

Gillie was too tired to dispute her. Now she was not only broke, she was in debt, and still there was no job in sight. How could she have done such a thing? It meant that any money she earned was not her own, and that she was obligated to Dulce no matter what happened.

Dulce yawned. "I'm starting to feel puffy-eyed. I knew it would catch up with me. Guess I'll go back to the old henhouse and take a nap."

They walked down West End Avenue. "Aren't you glad I was so alert, Gil girl?" Dulce crowed as they reached Ingram House. "You can take all the time you want paying me. I don't need it." She unlocked the door of their room and flung herself down on her bed.

Gillie hesitated. "I forgot to call the registry yesterday afternoon. I wonder if they're open on Sunday." She went back out to the hallway and dropped her dime into the telephone.

The registry was open but there had been no calls for her. Of course not. There had been none all week, and there never would be. And now she had acquired a hundred and fifty dollar debt.

It's lucky, she thought, that I learned how to type at college. Won't that be a nice career for Gillie, the ex-actress?

Chapter Nine

The Quick-Help Office Services agency was on Forty-first Street, near the theater district. It had been advertised in *Performers Only*. Probably most of their people were unemployed actors like herself.

Gillie chuckled ruefully as she stepped off the elevator. Was she an unemployed actress, or merely unemployed?

She filled out an application card and was given a typing test. Afterward, one of the men in charge explained the agency's system.

"We get these calls for temporary help from offices around town," he told her. "Employees go on vacation, see, or get sick, or there's extra work to do. At the end of the week you make out a time sheet of the hours you put in." He rummaged through his *In* box for a sample. "No counting lunch, now! Only the time you work. Have your supervisor sign it, give him a copy, and mail one to us. We'll send you your check."

"I could certainly use a check," Gillie said with a half-hearted smile.

"Want to go out on a job right now?"

"Today?"

It was Monday, only a day since she had realized she would have to take office work. But there could be no stalling now. She copied the address he gave her and left, stopping once on the way to call the registry.

For the rest of the day she typed a survey report for a furniture manufacturer. The job was to last two weeks.

Will I, wondered Gillie, last two weeks? Seven hours a day of *this?*

The week passed slowly, but on Saturday the furniture company faded into unimportance as she and Dulce packed their belongings for moving. Barney and Hovis came to help them. They loaded a taxi with suitcases, with Dulce's radio and fake fur scatter rugs. Dulce rode with the luggage while the others walked the four blocks to the new apartment.

"This is pretty good for me," said Dulce when their possessions were spread out on the sidewalk, "considering I've been at Ingram three whole months. You should have seen me leave college. After just one year it took a station wagon and two wardrobe trunks to get me home."

Within a few minutes they had moved everything up the stairs. While Dulce unpacked, Gillie made a grocery list. The boys were staying to dinner, and she and Dulce would need food for the weekend and a stock of basic supplies. The list grew enormous.

"Sugar?" Dulce called out. "Salt and pepper? Spices and stuff? Gee, I just remembered, Gil. Can you cook? I can't."

"I can get by," Gillie said. "But if I'm cooking, you're washing the dishes!"

They all walked out to Broadway together. After one look at the crowded supermarket, the boys decided to wait outside.

"Ooh, this is fun," squealed Dulce, seizing a cart. "We even have soft music piped through the aisles."

"And clacking females," said Gillie. "I thought that's what you wanted to get away from. At least the ones at Ingram House didn't shove."

When they returned to the street they found that the boys had passed their time at a bakery and bought a cake for dinner.

"We should have two and a half candles, one for each room," said Gillie.

"Which is the half?" Dulce asked. "The kitchen or the bathroom? They both seem fractional to me."

A door was open when they reached the second floor. In the doorway, arms folded, stood a middle-aged woman with cow-like eyes. She was stuffed unsuitably into a girlish cotton dress and ballet shoes.

"You just moved in upstairs?" she asked vaguely.

"We did." Dulce pointed to Gillie and herself. "The boys were helping us."

"How nice," the woman simpered. There was a trill in her soft, flat voice. "I'm Mrs. Mead. Lila Mead. I live right here underneath you. It's going to be nice having you girls for neighbors."

"I'm sure we'll enjoy it, too, Mrs. Mead." Dulce introduced herself and the others, and took another step toward the stairs.

"I'm glad the people who lived there before you, moved out," Mrs. Mead continued. "They were girls, too, just like you. There were three of them and they —were—so—*noisy*." She shook her head. "I'm not too sure they weren't thrown out. If they were, it might have been partly my fault, and I'm not one bit sorry. Every single night, I had to ring the super and complain. Morrison and I are business people. We have to get up at seven o'clock in the morning and we go to bed at eleven. Those girls would carry on—" Again she shook her head. "I don't know what they did. It sounded like a madhouse."

Gillie and Dulce clucked politely and all four went on up the stairs.

"Help!" Dulce exclaimed when they were behind their own closed door. "Is she all set to give us a hard time!"

Hovis, because he came from Texas, broiled the steak which had been bought to celebrate the occasion. Gillie made a salad and cooked the vegetables. They had frozen Hawaiian punch with dinner and espresso coffee with dessert.

As the dishes were cleared away, Gillie said, "I've

71

got to admit it, Dulce, you were right. This is the first decent meal I've had since I left home."

"You said it," Hovis agreed. "Don't be afraid to ask us again, any time."

Another week went by at the furniture company. She supposed there were people who spent their lives in such places. Did they really not mind it? Or did they have to do it anyway, whether they minded or not? How many of them had once had a dream, and failed, and ended up behind a typewriter in an office like this, knowing it was to be forever?

Faithfully, twice a day, she would call the Wynn Registry. What would they think of her, phoning with such desperate regularity, when obviously no producer was ever going to ask for her? But she had stubbornly kept her membership. She had to have hope.

On Thursday, after work, she stopped at Mr. Borisov's to order fifty more composites.

"You get any job with my peecture?" he asked.

"Not yet. I guess this is a bad time of year."

The photographer shrugged. "Every time of year bad time. You ever stop to think, there too many people in show business? That's the trahble. Why not get married, stay home with babies?"

"I *want* to be an actress."

"You and all the others." He sounded resigned. "You all in competition with each other. You be much happier you decide do something else. Crazy place, show business."

She left the studio, still more disheartened. Climbing the stairs to her apartment, she heard voices. Dulce and her boyfriends again. Gillie was not in the mood to face Dulce's boyfriends. She unlocked the door, planning to go straight to the bedroom and shut everyone out.

But Dulce sat alone on the sofa, sipping a glass of tangerine juice. She was watching a newscast on a gleaming, powder blue television set.

Gillie's eyes opened wide. "Where did it come from?"

"I bought it! Aren't you surprised, Gil?"

"Am I! Dulce, this is great! I've been perishing for one."

"Me, too. Do you realize that sometimes Barney's *on* TV? Maybe you will be, too, pretty soon. And there's me, with my sponsor contracts."

"Of course. You bought it on purpose to watch the commercials." Gillie sat down beside her. "Dulce, you're a peach. Isn't this fun? It cheers me up even though I had to spend money for more pictures today."

"Something tells me your investment isn't paying off. Haven't you gotten any calls yet?"

"No, and I never will."

"Oh, stop. Why don't you audition for TV?"

"Audition! I'd love to, but where? Who's ever holding auditions?"

"You could always go read for the casting director at NATV. Call him and make an appointment. I can't guarantee, of course. Most things are filmed in Hollywood. But if he has anything that suits you, well—at least he'll have seen you."

"Sounds like a long shot, but I'll try it," said Gillie. "I'll call him tomorrow."

Later that evening Gillie typed new résumés on a machine she had borrowed from Hovis. Dulce was still watching television, with the sound turned low. They had been reprimanded twice on other evenings for making noise after the Meads had gone to bed.

The phone rang. Gillie picked it up.

"Haven't you any consideration at all?" said Mrs. Mead, her voice still incongruously sugary. "What are you thinking of, using a *type*writer at *night?*"

"Oh, I'm sorry. I'll shut the windows."

From the sofa came a titter.

Gillie hung up. "Laugh all you want," she told her roommate. "You won't think it's so funny after we suffocate."

With the windows closed, the air was unbearably heavy. Gillie put a pillow under the typewriter and continued to work.

Dulce turned off the television. "Guess I'd better stop this noisy thing and take a bath. How will I run the water without its sounding like Niagara?"

"If I had any money," Gillie said, "I'd buy the old crab a pair of earplugs. But then she'd miss all the fun of bawling us out. No wonder those other girls left, the ones who were here before. They probably couldn't talk or walk or roll over in bed without our dream girl calling the police."

The room was quiet, except for the deliberately slow click of the typewriter. Their door buzzer rang with a shattering squawk.

Mrs. Mead stomped in. "What—is—the—matter—with—you—girls? You two are the most thoughtless, selfish—*type*writing, *this late at night!*"

"I have to," Gillie said. "It's part of my work."

"Your work! What work?"

"I'm an actress. I have to do this to get a job. And I've muffled everything so I don't see how you can possibly hear it."

"An actress!" snorted Mrs. Mead. "That's all you care about. Morrison and I are business people. We get up at seven o'clock, but do you care about that? An actress! And what about you?" She turned to Dulce. "You parade around all night with absolutely no consideration for others. Do you girls *live* at night?"

"Up until around midnight, yes," said Dulce.

Mrs. Mead's face became flushed with purple. "You're—you're—" She sputtered, gasping for breath. "You're *Bohemian!*"

While they stared in amazement, she marched from the room, slamming the door behind her. When the reverberations had died away, Gillie saw that her roommate was in a heap on the floor, shaking helplessly with laughter.

Before climbing into bed, Gillie went to the window and leaned on the sill, looking out. She gazed down into a sea of green leaves—the ailanthus trees that grew in the gardens below. Above them, up and down the alleyway, were yellow patches of windows. She heard laughter, faint music, and people calling to each other in Spanish.

At the end of the alley were two giant apartment buildings topped with looming water towers. In the half-dark, the fire escapes that climbed their sides appeared as iron grillwork balconies.

And the sky—not black or silvery blue like the sky over Mistra, it was deep rose pink and full of light. It glowed with the aliveness of the city beneath it, so different from the bare dark of night in the country. She was part of this city. She would never leave it now. She loved and belonged to New York.

Chapter Ten

Gillie wished it were her own mother coming that day, instead of Dulce's. Mom would be impressed by the wonderful apartment and the way the girls were managing on their own. Mrs. Rodgers, by Dulce's account, would only be critical.

And me? thought Gillie. What will she think of me? She'll think I'm provincial and unsophisticated, which I suppose I am. And I hope she doesn't have any inkling that I owe her daughter money.

Wearily she put away the dust mop. She would need a shower after all that cleaning. It was wretched, getting up at seven on a Saturday, but with Mrs. Rodgers coming, one had to be prepared.

The door opened and Dulce came in, dragging the loaded grocery cart. Perched on top was a gaily decorated bakery box.

"I bought tarts. She wants to take us out to lunch, but I figure you and I can have these when she leaves. We'll need them."

"You make your mother sound perfectly delightful," said Gillie.

"I don't *mind* her. It's just that I wish she wouldn't try to run my life."

At a punctual eleven-thirty the doorbell rang. Dulce hung over the stair rail as her mother climbed the two flights. "Strike number one," she whispered to Gillie. "No elevator."

"And no doorman."

Gillie was surprised at Mrs. Rodgers' unpatrician appearance. She was dumpy and she walked with a waddle. Her face, which was dominated by thick, dark eyebrows, seemed to hold the world at arm's length.

She collapsed, puffing, into the armchair. "Dulce, did you know the downstairs door was open when I came?"

"Open?" said Dulce.

"Unlocked. I didn't have to wait for the release bell."

"It does that sometimes. It gets a little warped in the humidity."

"Have you spoken to the janitor? I think it should be mended at once. This isn't safe, you know. The door should always be kept locked for your protection."

"It usually is," said Dulce meekly. "It just sticks now and then, but nothing ever happens."

Mrs. Rodgers sat up. "I should *hope* not. I noticed

quite a few rundown streets nearby as I taxied up from the station. Now, Broadway out there looks terrible."

"Oh, you probably came through Central Park. A lot of those streets between Broadway and the park are rather depressed, but nothing ever—"

"I noticed a good deal of poverty on this side of Broadway, too, Dulce."

"Mother, which way did you *come*? This street's perfectly middle-class, honestly. And so's Eighty-sixth, and so's— In fact, Eighty-sixth is—"

"We'll talk about it later," said Mrs. Rodgers, becoming suddenly bland and amiable. "After we've had lunch. Are you ready, girls?"

They rode in a taxi both ways and ate an expensive luncheon of unhurried elegance at a smörgåsbord restaurant. Gillie felt she had seen another side of life, and yet all this was a matter of course for some people.

"I meant it when I told her this was the most fun I've had in New York," Gillie exclaimed after Mrs. Rodgers had left. "She'll never have to argue *me* into going out again. If she ever wants me, that is. Dulce, what's the matter? Did you eat too much?"

"I'm glad you enjoyed it," said Dulce in a deadened voice. "Gil, that was sweet of you to go off for a while and pretend you had errands."

"I thought you and your mother might want to talk."

Dulce nodded. "It was sweet of you. I mean that. Only trouble was, it backfired. Oh, no, don't start getting upset. I'm sure she would have come out with it anyway."

"Come out with what? Dulce, what happened? Did she say you couldn't see Barney?"

"I never mentioned Barney, and I'm glad you didn't either. He's much too unusual for Mother. No, dear, it isn't that. It's even worse. I could go on seeing Barney anyway, and she'd never know. It's about the apartment." Her face twisted tragically. "She doesn't want me to live here any more."

"*What?* But—how—but you signed the lease!"

"I know. Mother said I either break the lease, or I'm on my own financially, starting now. Gil, you know how much I make. I signed up for this place, counting on being subsidized. How would we manage?"

"But what's the matter with the apartment?"

"You heard her. She thinks we're in mortal danger. My mother thinks any street not paved with millionaires must be a slum full of crime. Which is silly, because *we* aren't millionaires."

"Why did she approve of Ingram House? That was more rundown than this."

"But you see, Ingram House was protected. It had a front door that locked, and a mother hen to watch over it. Oh, darn, Gil, that door's nearly always locked. Why does it have to stick just when Mother comes? I bet Mrs. Mead jinxed it on purpose. I hope

the next people who live here are six howling
banshees with granite feet."

"Dulce, are we really moving out?"

If they broke up the apartment, Gillie would have
to go home, back to Mistra. She could not stay on by
herself without any money. She hadn't even enough
for Ingram House any more.

"I haven't even paid for the television yet!" Dulce
cried. "I charged it. How am I supposed to pay for
it out of my salary?"

"I wish my salary were more," Gillie murmured.
"Then I could—"

"You know?" said Dulce, "I bet the door and the
neighborhood are just excuses. I bet my mother
doesn't think I'm old enough to have my own apartment. For land sakes, Gillie, I'm twenty-one!"

Gillie was silent while Dulce paced to the windows, back and forth.

"I bet when my children are in college," Dulce
continued, her voice rising shrilly, "she'll think I'm
too young to wear lipstick. I believe I'll marry a New
Zealander, and once a year Daddy can visit me there.
Oh, Gillie, what can I do? I won't go back home and
I won't go back to Ingram House, and that's final.
Just a minute." She seized an envelope from the
wastebasket, hunted for a pencil, and began figuring.

Gillie said, "If we break the lease, we won't get
back our deposit."

Dulce waved her hand for quiet. After a few mo-
ments she set down the pencil. "I'm staying."

You're staying, but what about me? Gillie wanted to ask. You won't know how to live on what you make. You'll need all the rest of the money I owe you just to pay for the TV set.

"I know she thought her little threat would get me out of here," said Dulce. "But she didn't reckon with the new me. Gillie, I'm going to be all on my own from now on. A real, live working girl, living on my salary. Boy!" Her eyes were dreamy and glowing. "I feel as if I were walking on bubbles. Isn't it great to be independent?"

Gillie managed to smile. "I guess it depends on what's the most important to you, money with strings attached, or—nothing. I think you can feel just as trapped by not having enough."

She turned away, thinking. On Monday she would begin a new job which the Quick-Help agency had assigned her. During her lunch hours she would have to look for something permanent and better paid. And that, once she had it, would mean no more time to make the rounds, no more opportunity to audition.

She went into the bedroom to be alone. Dulce was happy. For her, it would be like playing house, seeing if she could get along on her income. She would enjoy pinching pennies for a while. It would be new, and it would delight her to know that she did not need her parents' help. But Gillie? Gillie, who had come to New York so certain that the theater would open up for her—Gillie was now to be another clerk-typist. Her last chance gone. The dream was over.

Chapter Eleven

This time the agency sent her to an export office. She typed promotion letters to all parts of the world— Europe, the Orient, Africa.

Her desk faced a window that looked out over the Battery. She could see the Statue of Liberty in the morning sun; sparkling water and seagulls, ferry boats, and barges that carried whole freight cars.

Her boss was Robert O. Deckter. The Deckter Company was his own firm and he and Gillie were the only people in the office. He would lean on his elbow and watch her while she typed. It did not matter how often she told him she wasn't really an actress. He still thought she was glamorous, and was impressed by her.

She did not tell Dulce about this. Dulce would have misunderstood, imagining romance, as usual. But Mr. Deckter's admiration was not romantic. He was a family man with pictures of the children on his desk. He simply enjoyed what seemed to him a sugar-frosted employee. She left the office every day on floating feet.

Am I really as glamorous as all that? she wondered. *Me?*

On Thursday of her first week, he asked her if she would like to stay on permanently.

"It would only be part-time," he said. "I wouldn't have enough to keep you busy a full day, but you could work mornings or afternoons, whichever is better for you."

He offered to pay the agency's fee, which was required when any of their jobs became permanent.

Gillie promised to think it over. She loved the office, but part-time work would mean so little income.

As the day wore on she weighed the offer again and again. Perhaps this was her answer. In her time off she could go on looking for an acting job. There was her debt to pay, but—

I will fall for this temptation, she decided. As long as Dulce keeps saying she doesn't need the money, I won't sacrifice everything to get it for her. When she does, I'll find a Saturday job, but I can't give up the theater.

The apartment was deserted when she reached home that evening. Dulce had a dinner date with one of her Ivy League men. How soon would it be before she grew serious enough to settle down and marry one of them? She still dated Barney more than anyone else, but, just as she had intended, their relationship remained casual.

This, it seemed to Gillie, was true genius. How did it happen? What cosmic order directed Dulce's life, while her own was left in chaos?

"I never even know which way to turn," Gillie muttered to herself. "Nothing ever works out for me. No matter what I do, a door slams in my face. Even Mr. Deckter—I know I can't live on a part-time salary. Why did I tell him yes?"

While watching television, she munched on scraps from the refrigerator. She did not even feel like cooking.

It was nine o'clock when the phone rang. On hearing Barney's voice she began automatically, "I'm sorry, Dulce's out. Can I have her call you—"

"Baby, who cares? I was calling you."

"Me?"

"I'm letting you in on a big secret. There's this off-Broadway show I happen to know about, that's casting now. It wasn't mentioned in *Performers Only* so you'd never hear of it in time if it wasn't for me."

She felt a chill of excitement. "What is it?"

"I don't know, some crazy thing about a guy with a mother complex. His stepfather gets upset and has him committed."

"A psychological drama?"

"Yeah. It's called *The Shores of Isolation*. The author's a businessman who had to get the Great American Play off his chest. He's producing it himself. It'll be a small production, but it's paid work. There

are a lot of bit parts, patients in the hospital, so you
might be lucky. Tomorrow afternoon."

"Tomorrow! But I'm working."

"So knock off early. Why miss a chance?" He gave
her the time and place.

The audition was being held in a shabby cellar
playhouse on the Lower East Side. She took a seat
on one of the folding chairs that dotted the floor, and
studied her fellow actors. Some were tense, some were
meditating or entering a mood, but no one appeared
panic-stricken, as she was.

Her eyes rested on a young man sitting by himself,
paging through a script. She started. It was Ralph
Costa. Of course, if Barney had known, Ralph would,
too. She looked for Barney and Hovis, but they were
not there.

Ralph was walking toward her. "Hi." He stopped
by her chair. "Barney said you might be coming.
What's new?"

"Oh . . . nothing much. What's new with you?"

"About the same. Be seeing you. Good luck."

Fear surged up inside her. Why did this have to
happen? Why couldn't she at least hide in anonym-
ity at her first public audition? Now she could not
possibly read without thinking of Ralph out there
watching her.

They were talented people, beautiful people. They
read with polished craftsmanship. The other girls,

though hardly celebrities, looked, dressed, and carried themselves as though they were. And they were beautiful. An actress had to give that impression. She had to be sure of herself.

Gillie's fear grew stronger. She almost stopped breathing. Ralph had gone up to the stage and she realized that he was already cast. She remembered what Barney had said about the play. "A guy with a mother complex."

The "guy" was the central character. Ralph was the guy. He was the lead, the star of the play, while she had only come to try out for a bit part which she would never get. He would laugh at her.

"Ralph, take that scene where you're dishing it out to the nurse, page eighty-three," called the director. He was a thin, arty-looking person. Gillie stared idly, wondering how anyone's face could be so long and narrow. He was whispering to a large, blond man in a Brooks Brothers suit, who was seated next to him. That must be the author.

Why did she keep letting her mind wander instead of listening to the play?

More people read, some again and again for different roles. Barney had been right about the many bit parts. But they were difficult. How could you portray the mentally ill when you had never seen how they behaved and how they looked? The others all seemed to know. Did you roll your eyes, the way a girl had done at college for Ophelia's mad scene?

Goodness, no, it was far more subtle than that. But how? She watched, and still she did not know.

The room was cooled by fans, but they were not helping her. The others, easy and poised, had nothing to fear. They knew what to do and they were doing it well.

Her back was damp. She touched her face and it was sticky. Stealthily she pulled out her compact. The mirror caught a light and flashed, and people stared.

Gillie closed her eyes. She was going to die then and there, or else be sick. How did people get through auditions? *How did they do it?*

The play sounded crazy. It would not be much of a production anyway, here in this cellar. But what else was there?

There was the Deckter Company. She liked working for Mr. Deckter. Some evening she would come and see this play, because Ralph was in it, and she would go backstage afterward and congratulate him.

Her gloves were on her hands, her purse was clasped tightly, and she had risen. Concentrating only on the door ahead of her, she left.

The street outside was alive with children playing and old women sitting on chairs in front of their tenement houses. The air had its usual gritty haze, but it seemed fresh and clear, now that she was free. She no longer had to dread her turn upon the stage, stumbling through a part she could not possibly play.

She was lost, and had to ask a policeman where to find the subway. As she waited on the platform, blasted by the roar of a passing express train, she felt sure she was going to cry. Where did all the others get their looks, their poise, their talent and experience? How senseless she had been, taking every cent of her money to come to New York and act when she hadn't a chance. Mr. Borisov was right. There were too many people in show business. Far too many, and they were all better than she was, and prettier, and unafraid.

Chapter Twelve

Almost as though she had imagined it, yesterday's audition was fading from Gillie's mind. This was reality: standing here in their little kitchen and making sandwiches for the housewarming party that evening. Behind her, Dulce straightened up the living room.

She made stripy sandwiches, alternating white and wholewheat bread, then quartered them and cut off their crusts. She made open sandwiches with watercress on cream cheese, and garnished crackers with anchovies or dabs of cheap caviar.

"Holy smoke!" she burst out at last. "Nobody's going to eat all this. Not at an after-dinner party."

"Better to have too much than too little," Dulce said.

"And punch with strawberries floating in it. You'd think—"

Dulce gasped. "Strawberries? Did you say strawberries? Gil, I forgot to buy them!"

"You'd think it was a wedding," Gillie continued,

"instead of a housewarming. All we need are the men."

"They'll be here. And we almost have a preacher. One of the boys is a divinity student." Dulce picked up her purse and started out. "I'm off for strawberries. I'll get flowers, too, for the table."

The two girls sat in the living room looking at each other. The table was laid, the punch had all but the ice in it, and the cream cheese on the open sandwiches was beginning to crack.

"It's nowhere near eight-thirty yet," said Dulce. "And besides, they'll all be late. People are always late to parties."

"We shouldn't have gotten ready so soon. It wasn't smart after all. We should have left some odds and ends to keep us busy. This is awful." Gillie smoothed out her skirt.

The buzzer rang and Dulce jumped from her chair. The first guests who trickled in sat stiffly, embarrassed strangers trying to talk to one another. Only as the room began to fill did the party relax.

Gillie's heart bumped when she saw Barney, Ralph, and Hovis in the doorway. After yesterday, she had dreaded their coming. What would they say to her about the audition? They were confident actors and would never understand.

In the course of passing around glasses of punch, she found herself next to Ralph.

"Hey," he said. "What happened to you yesterday? They wanted to hear you read."

She stared at him. Who did? He was making fun of her.

"After you left," he persisted. "They asked about you. You didn't even stay around and read. You should have told them if you had to be somewhere."

"But—me? Are you sure it was me?"

"Sure, I'm sure. They said that tall girl in the blue dress and they pointed to your empty chair."

Idiotically she shook her head. "They can't have meant me. How did they know I was there? I didn't even read."

"Well, you weren't invisible. *I* saw you, and so did Fred and Corny. Director and author," he explained. "They had a part they wanted you to try, a girl in the hospital. It's a short scene but a good one. If I were you, I'd call them first thing Monday morning."

"I— Are you sure?"

He smiled. "Don't take my word for it. Call the director. You'd better start about nine o'clock and keep trying until you catch him. I don't know when he'll get in. It's Fred Wales. I'll give you the number." He set down his glass and rustled through his pocket.

How crazy. How absolutely, madly crazy, she thought, as she put Fred's number in the bedroom for safe keeping.

When Gillie returned to the guests, Dulce whispered, "He's a doll, isn't he?"

"Who?"

"Ralph! Isn't that why you're sailing around in the clouds? I saw him dating you up."

A laugh too big for Gillie's throat choked out in a wild squeak. "Dulce, you're nuts with your one-track mind. It wasn't anything like that. I'll tell you tomorrow, but not now. I don't want to wake up too soon."

Mr. Deckter was impressed as she began her series of phone calls. At last, at a quarter past eleven, she was able to talk to Fred Wales.

"Oh, yes," said the director. "Yes, I remember you. Can you come and see me this afternoon?"

For the rest of the time, until one o'clock, she typed with trembling hands. She looked out the window at the ships. They made no impression. She hardly saw the beautiful harbor. All morning she was on the verge of saying to Mr. Deckter, "Don't you realize, if by some wild accident I ever did get a part in a show, I'd have to leave you?"

But she did not say it. Of course she would not get the part, and she did not want to talk about it. She wanted to hold it to herself a while longer.

This time she did not even see the children and the old women as she walked toward the theater. She saw, in her mind, only the stage, and she was on it, reading. Afterward she would go home, and to-

morrow she would be back as usual with Mr. Deckter, nothing changed.

The script was in her hand and she was staring
at it. Mr. Wales was telling her about the part.

"This girl's a schizophrenic," he said. "Do you know
what that is?"

She could not remember her own name, so how
could she remember what a schizophrenic was?

"The schizophrenic," he continued, "is a person
who's lost his grip on reality. His personality has become so disintegrated that he can't relate to the outside world. He lives inside himself, sometimes with-
drawn and sometimes active, but in a way that
hasn't much to do with what's going on around him.
This girl's been sitting through some of the other
scenes, as quiet as part of the background. She
doesn't respond when she's spoken to. But here she
has an outburst. Much of what the patients say is
symbolic of the whole play, which is a diatribe
against conformity."

Gillie remembered the clean-cut man in the Brooks
Brothers suit. A diatribe against conformity? From
him?

Cued by Mr. Wales, she read through the scene.
She had little idea of what the lines were about,
but she tried to feel like the girl she was playing—
a girl who could have been anyone, even Gillie, sup-
pressed by what she considered unfair authority, cry-
ing out for the freedom to be herself. She remembered Saint Joan's speech to the inquisitors in Shaw's

play, which she had practiced in her room long ago, when she had first thought she must become an actress.

The part she was reading consisted of four short lines and a speech half a page long, double spaced. She finished it, hardly daring to remember where she was. Auditioning for a play? It was her first real chance, and could very well be her last.

Mr. Wales called, "Bill, you got a minute?"

The stage manager came forward to listen and Gillie read the scene again.

"Can you come back at five-thirty?" said Mr. Wales. "Corny Avedon'll be here then."

She had reached the street before she thought to look at her watch. It was a little after three. What did all this mean? Did she have the part? Did they like her? She stumbled into a movie theater to wait out the two long hours.

Corny, or Cornell, Avedon was dressed as modishly as he had been at the audition. With his tan attaché case he was a picture of Madison Avenue. Did Ralph know him? Was that how he had gotten the lead? More likely Ralph knew Fred Wales.

She was glad she had gone to the movies instead of worrying about the part. It was still fresh to her. When the reading was over they asked her about herself, about her experience, and her reaction to the role.

"I like it," she said, unsure of what they wanted.

95

"No, I mean how do you feel about the girl?" said Mr. Wales. "What's going through your mind when you read the scene?"

Gillie told them about *Saint Joan*. Mr. Avedon looked puzzled, but Mr. Wales understood.

They thanked her. "Glad you got in touch with us," said Mr. Wales. "Corny thought you looked like just the girl he had in mind. Rehearsals begin in a couple of weeks. You'll be called."

Mr. Avedon shook hands with her, and Gillie went out to the street.

She was bumped, pushed, and pinched in the subway, for it was rush hour, but she barely noticed. It might have been somebody else they were jostling, or a sack of flour. Who cared? They were lovely people. They were her audience.

Chapter Thirteen

Neither had any money for celebrating, but Gillie
and Dulce ate by candlelight that evening and pretended it was a party.

Dulce said, "Nuts to Mother's purse strings. We're
going to be sitting pretty."

"Not financially!" Gillie replied with a giggle.
"I'll be making even less than I did typing. But think
of it, you're living with an actress. Why, I might
amount to something someday!"

On her last Friday with Mr. Deckter he took her
to lunch at Fraunces Tavern, where George Washington had held a farewell dinner for his troops.

"We'll have ours here, too," he said. "Eat hearty.
You might not get another chance, from what I hear
about the acting profession."

"I know," said Gillie. "I've had experience with
that part of it already."

The next day she received another clipping from
her mother. She had written home in her first de-
lirium after getting the part. Mom must have trotted
right down to the newspaper, letter and all, and had

even given them one of Gillie's pictures to use.

The picture was her laughing pose in the black wool cape. Gillie blinked in unbelieving admiration. She looked stunning. She got out Betty's wedding clipping and compared them.

There was no comparison. Betty was all the other brides who had ever been on that page since the paper was founded. How narrowly Gillie had escaped such a commonplace fate. She held Betty's clipping up to the light so that the advertisement on the other side showed grotesquely through her face.

"Now what have you got to say to the girl you conned, thinking you were being so smart?" she said aloud. "Well, you can have him, Babyface, and all that goes with him. It's not for me. What do I want with the junior partner of a small-town hardware store, when I can have this?"

She read through her own article. It was just what she had expected. No mention was made of the disappointments, the failures, the defeats. Mistra's daughter had gone forth to become an actress, and she had become one. Even her work in the summer theater and in school plays was exaggerated.

Satisfied, she put away Betty's clipping and set about making a bulletin board of corrugated cardboard, which she fastened to the wall above her bed. With an old corsage pin—she believed it had been a corsage from Jim—she anchored her first publicity story to the center of the board. It would grow old and brown, but she would have it there to look at always, even when rainy days came again.

Once more she walked the dingy streets to the cellar playhouse, but this time it felt different. She was going to a place where she belonged.

For the first rehearsal they sat in a circle to read their parts. She listened passively to the others, trying to picture a man like Cornell Avedon writing such a play. It was hard, too, to imagine Ralph as the weak neurotic he portrayed. Yet he did it well—so well that he was not even Ralph any more, but Ben, the boy in the story.

When her own turn came she felt suddenly self-conscious. She was, after all, an amateur. How many of these others had never acted before in New York? But she kept *Saint Joan* in mind and no one criticized her.

Did I say amateur? she thought. I'm professional. A professional actress!

She repeated it, but was not quite convinced. It was too fantastic.

After the rehearsal, she found herself walking out to the street with Ralph.

"I meant to tell you," she said. "I think it's wonderful that you got that part. And you do it perfectly."

"I'm not exactly doing anything yet," he told her. "This isn't what anybody'd call a performance. You might not even recognize me by the time we get to the previews. But thanks for saying nice things."

"Previews? Like a movie?"

"It's the same as the out-of-town tryouts Broadway shows have, only ours are right here. It's about three or four performances."

"Who comes?"

"Anybody. Tickets are usually a little cheaper, that's all. And the critics keep their hands off until the opening. Hey—feel like having a cup of coffee?"

"I'd love it."

She was surprised to find a shiny diner in the middle of the slums. With block after block of poverty, this area was like the edge of the world. She looked out the window beside their table, pensively watching a hopscotch game as she murmured her order for iced coffee.

"You know," she said, "I've heard about the Lower East Side before, but I never imagined what it looked like. Around Mistra, where I come from, there are a few broken-down houses, but nothing like this. I guess, even though I've been here two and a half months, I still don't know New York."

"There's a lot of it," said Ralph. "A lot of different things to see."

After a while she asked, "Are you a native New Yorker?"

"Nope. New Haven. The street I lived on might remind you of this."

She was jarred to hear him say it so frankly, and a

little embarrassed. No wonder he did not mind the way he lived now. He was used to it.

"New Haven?" she asked. "Is that where you got the theater bug? From the out-of-town openings?"

"That's where I should have been bitten, isn't it? Actually it was much later. I never really knew what I wanted to do. When I got out of the Navy I came here to try some college, and that's when things started happening. Remember Marsha Greenfield, at our party?"

"Mm," said Gillie shortly.

"I met Marsha through some friends, and we talked a lot about the theater. She was in a show then, a little no-pay affair. She happened to know the fellow who was producing it, so when they needed a replacement, she got me in. After that I was hopeless."

While he ordered a second cup, she tamped at her ice cubes with her spoon. Why was it so unpleasant to hear that Marsha had been the one to get Ralph into the theater? Why did Gillie have to mind so acutely being the stranger?

"Have you given up college completely?" she asked.

"Hope not. Someday I mean to go back and study some more. But not until I get a better start in acting. I feel I can study any time. It's getting into acting that's hard."

"You can say that again."

They left the diner and went on to the subway.

Before she could pull a token out of her change purse, Ralph had dropped one into the turnstile for her.

"You say you haven't seen much of the city yet?" he asked as they waited on the platform. "How much?"

She told him. As far north as Ninety-sixth Street, as far south as the Battery. The Lower East Side, the area where Ralph lived, Greenwich Village only once—and her memory of that was topsy-turvy, for she had gotten lost on its crooked streets.

"How does Sunday look in your datebook? You free?"

The train came roaring in. Above its noise he shouted, "I can show you some more of our sights. Pick you up at two?"

It's my first date since I've been here, she thought as she dressed on Sunday. My first—since Jim.

How odd it was. She had wondered if she would ever again be able to bear going out with another man. But now she was not only bearing it, she was looking forward to it. She was glad he had asked her.

They took the subway to the familiar Battery stop. There he led her into the ferry terminal where they went through a turnstile and boarded the boat.

"This is the first time I've been on a ferryboat," Gillie told him. "Where are we going?"

"Staten Island, and back again. We're going for

the trip, not especially for the island. Unless you want to look around when we get there."

"What's it like?"

"Nice countryside."

"If we don't look around Staten Island, what will we do?"

"Look around Manhattan."

"I think I'd rather do that. I've seen plenty of countryside."

She felt the heartbeat of the engines and watched the boat begin to move. As they drew away from the pier, she looked up and saw the office building where she had worked with Mr. Deckter. One of those windows had been hers.

Ralph pointed out the famous downtown buildings and showed her the Brooklyn Bridge and Governor's Island. They passed the Statue of Liberty, standing proud and alone in the water. Now the skyline of lower Manhattan was gray and jagged and magical, as she had seen it in pictures. When it was far away, they walked to the front of the boat to watch the hills of Staten Island rise up ahead of them.

The engines went off and with a crunching and grinding the boat was docked. They crossed the gangplank into the pier, which was almost a city in itself. Like the Port Authority Bus Terminal, it was full of shops and snack bars. From the building's entrance they looked out into the streets, and

then went back to a luncheonette for coffee. Afterward, they boarded a ferry for the return.

She watched Manhattan come closer and closer.
Despite its bulky stone strangeness, she felt that she
was coming home. How odd that she, who had once
thought she would miss the farms and the green-
ness of grass and trees, should call this home. It was
such a queer man-made place, with its pink night
sky, where a street lined with spindly saplings
seemed as lush as a jungle.

The boat bumped again into dock and they
stepped off.

"Sometime I'll have to try this in the evening,"
Gillie said.

She had not meant it as a hint, but Ralph replied:
"We'll do that. We'll go off just at sundown, and
that'll bring us back as it's getting dark. You should
see all this in the dark, after the lights go on." He
waved his arm to take in the tip of Manhattan. "I'm
glad you like this trip, Gillie. I always have."

They took a subway to Greenwich Village and
walked along West Fourth Street, looking into the
windows of minuscule shops that sold handmade
jewelry and leatherwork. They walked back and
forth, for she could not get enough of the Village.
She loved the old, small houses, sleepy and charming—almost all that was left of a quieter era.

They walked up Christopher Street, from Village
Square to Sheridan Square, and down West Fourth
again until they stopped at a lunchroom. While they

split a hero sandwich and a Coke, he showed her tickets someone had given him for another off-Broadway show that night.

She counted up the hours she would have spent with him before the day was over. More than ten. Almost half a day with Ralph Costa, and it was wonderful. Every minute of it.

Chapter Fourteen

The dressing room was crowded, stuffy, and hot.
Outdoors it was nearly the end of October, but no
autumn air found its way inside. Even if it had, it
would have made little difference. Who could help
feeling feverish on a night such as this—the first of
their preview performances?

Some of the girls talked nervously; one sang to
herself. Most of them made up in silence, praying
that they and the play would be successful.

As she carefully smoothed on a pallid greasepaint,
Gillie tried to forget the play and remember only
the good times she had had with Ralph. On their
second date he had come to her apartment. The four
of them—Dulce, Barney, Ralph, and herself—had
made popcorn on the kitchen stove and toasted
marshmallows on shish-kebab skewers over candle
flames.

Another time, giddy with their steady, if low, sal-
aries, they had gone Dutch treat on a trip to Bear
Mountain to see the autumn leaves changing color.

He's such fun, she thought, paling out her lipstick with clown white. He likes to do things, not just sit around and make silly small talk. And he's so *real*.

She had already met a number of men in New York—the actors in her company, the boys at Barney's party, and most of Dulce's dates. So many of them had seemed artificial and sophisticated. Ralph was not like that. He was the most sincere person in the world. He was so sincere that sometimes Barney laughed at him, telling him not to take life so hard.

A glowing warmth filled her as she thought of Ralph, and it helped to calm the quivering she felt in every nerve. She must keep her mind on Ralph and not on the play. She would try to relive the Bear Mountain trip from beginning to end. That should help distract her.

But it did not work. All she could think of was Ralph in the next dressing room, preparing to go on in the leading role. This play was giving him his first big part. He was probably as nervous as she was.

She looked at herself in the mirror. What an ashen-white character she was playing! Ashen in looks, but violent in behavior. It was the sort of part Marsha could do with ease.

Gillie remembered a television show she had seen two weeks before. Ralph had told her that Marsha was starring in an experimental half-hour drama for new actors and playwrights. Marsha had capitalized on her not-so-chic appearance to play a slatternly

young woman whom nobody loved. She had per-
formed like a real pro, with no stiffness, no inhibi-
tions, no straining—all the things that plagued Gillie
in her present role. Marsha was lucky. That was the
kind of person she naturally was.

But if Marsha gets the parts that are Marsha, Gillie thought, why can't I get the parts that are me?

"Five minutes," someone called. Gillie froze. She
caught sight of her own eyes staring from the mirror
as she swallowed the fear that had crept up from
her stomach and clamped around her throat.

"Places!"

She was not in the first act. She could only wait
in the dressing room. From out in front she heard
the rasp of the curtains sliding open.

Still as a rock, she sat on the stage, a sick girl sur-
rounded by people she neither saw nor heard. What
did the world seem like to this girl?

It was something she should have figured out long
ago. She should be living in that world now, instead
of thinking of Dulce, Barney, and Hovis, and dozens
of others out there watching.

The time was approaching for Gillie to come to life.
Was it Gillie, or the girl she was playing? Of course
it was the girl. Gillie did not exist.

She heard her cue. Now she was speaking and she
knew it was hopeless. It was only Gillie playing a
role, trying to do it as best she could.

She sat down again, her speaking part over. She

could not fool herself. Even while it was going on, she had felt the flatness, the deadness of it. There was nothing left, not even *Saint Joan*. Maybe by opening night . . .

She worked hard during the next two days, but still it was wrong. What had happened to all the terror and passion she had felt in the beginning? Had she done it too often? Had the rehearsals taken away all her feelings? That meant she was not a true actress, if rehearsals could kill her performance.

"You go back to sleep," said Dulce as she dressed for work on the day the play was to open. "Quit stewing over that part. You did a magnificent job. For now, I suggest you take it easy or you'll be the limpest thing on stage."

"What do you know about it?" croaked Gillie. "Even if you do work for a television network? Oh, Dulce, you never saw it at the readings. I was *good*. I know I was, and now it's all gone."

"You must be okay or they would have thrown you out, I should think."

"I'm probably not important enough to bother with."

Unable to sleep, she got up and made breakfast for Dulce. Loyal Dulce, who could hardly stand the play, who considered it sick and pretentious, was going to see it again that night. She was only going because of Gillie.

This time there were to be critics out front. It was hard to imagine critics bothering with a cellar on the Lower East Side, but they did.

Gillie struggled over her make-up, smudging it, removing it, reapplying it.

The girl next to her whispered, "Nice we don't have too much to say, isn't it? I never was a good study."

"I can learn my lines all right," Gillie answered, her throat dry as a cornfield in November. "But I get out on the stage and I'm sure I've forgotten them. It's my long speech that scares me."

"Aw, it's okay. Just don't let your voice crack the way it did last night. You shouldn't strain. If you don't feel it, play it in a lower key, but don't strain."

The first act was over. She felt ill and wanted to run. She wanted to be home with Mom and Dad, safe in her little room.

A hand touched her shoulder. "Take it easy, kid." It was Ralph.

Gillie managed a grateful smile. "Thanks, Ralph," she whispered. "And loads of luck. I think you're just terrific."

She took her place and the curtains opened. How odd it was to be watched by drama critics. These were real drama critics, so unlike small-town reporters with their words of praise for everybody.

She had nothing to say in the second act, and nothing to do but try to feel lonely and afraid.

When the scene was over, Fred met her backstage.

"You're not bad," he said, "but you aren't coming over enough. You've got to project it more. And in the next one, when you have your speaking part, *please* give it all you've got. That's a pivotal scene. It's got to have punch."

Don't strain . . . give it all you've got . . . take it easy . . . project it more. How on earth could you project withdrawal? Gillie went into the dressing room to repair her make-up. Fred was not satisfied with her. She couldn't blame him.

"Okay, kids," the stage manager called. It was time for the third act.

She hear her cue. Ralph was saying, "Who is it that has shut us in here? Who has the right to decide that we should be in and the rest outside?"

"We *are* outside," she cried. "It is the rest who are shut in. Bound."

She wanted to laugh. This, coming from Cornell Avedon, with his suburban mansion and socialite wife? She spoke her lines mechanically and knew they sounded exactly that: mechanical.

There was a party after the play. Gillie met Mrs. Avedon, who had thought the whole thing was silly right from the beginning, and still did. But Corny was pleased with himself. He must have fulfilled a secret yearning when *The Shores of Isolation* reached the stage.

It was a nervous party, for the reviews were not yet out. Gillie grew sleepy, but she was determined to stay. She would stay as long as Ralph did, though she had hardly a chance to talk to him. He was everybody's now, not her friend alone.

At last someone came in with an armload of newspapers. There was a rush for the theater page.

"The author, in his first work, shows ability, though uneven skill," somebody read aloud.

"The hospital scenes are staged in such a way as to emphasize the isolated madness of each character," read another.

"As the young man, victimized by a neurotic attachment, Ralph Costa is sensitive and likeable."

"Ralph Costa portrays Ben with great sensitivity—"

"As Ben, Mr. Costa is convincingly bewildered and angry—"

Oh, Ralph, Ralph, they liked you! You're a success!

Through the cluster of people she managed to send him a proud smile.

She wrote a letter home. "Dear Mom, Dad, Jean, and Ward. We opened, and I guess we'll last for a while. This fellow I told you about—Ralph—got the best reviews. They all adored him even if they weren't wild about the play. I don't know how much this is going to do for my career, but it's experience. I guess it helps a lot to be able to say you were in a show in New York . . ."

She read it over and wished it were not such a tepid letter. But what else could she say? She could not tell her own family that she felt flatter than a popped balloon.

Chapter Fifteen

In three weeks it was all over. The play closed. When the news was announced there were murmurs of dismay, but no one seemed surprised.

The day after the last performance Gillie walked to the park. She sat on a bench by the river and listened to the cries of seagulls. Wind tossed the water into whitecaps. It was a sparkling day, so lovely she felt like an outsider looking in, trying to share the beauty and the fun.

"Now what?" she asked the New Jersey shore. "What happens to me now? Do I look for another acting job? Do I find one? I sure didn't make much of a hit with this. Do I go back to Mr. Deckter in the meantime? He probably has another girl by now. I've paid what I owed to Dulce, but I'm still flat broke. Do I starve? Do I borrow?"

A woman passing by with her poodle gave Gillie a wary look, and she realized she had been talking out loud.

Soon there was a letter from Mom, answering hers about the closing of the play. They wanted her to come home for Thanksgiving.

"That'd be fun for you," Dulce said when Gillie told her about it in the evening. "I bet Thanksgiving at your place is real nice and homey. What's the matter, don't you want to go?"

"I'd love to see the folks again, but—oh, Dulce, I couldn't get through it. I couldn't spend the week trying to pretend everything's fine when it isn't."

"But you got into a play! They were thrilled about that."

"Yes, and the play fell on its face and so did I. Don't you see? I thought big things would happen to me, and they haven't. I spent all summer getting a part half a page long that I couldn't even handle."

"Some people spend much longer than that and get nowhere."

Gillie could not deny that this was true. She had indeed been lucky to find a part so soon. It was terrible, listening to other hopefuls and hearing how long they had been making the rounds.

"But I failed. That's what gets me. I think it's myself I can't face, when I used to be so sure."

"Well then, prove to yourself how good you are by going up there and acting like the toast of Broadway."

Gillie was still reluctant to go home and pretend. It was all right, at a distance, if they did not know what was happening, but she could not be with them and keep up the lie. She wrote that she did not have enough money to make the trip.

Her father sent her a check for the fare. Now she had to go. Somehow she would manage, and somehow leave them with the illusion that their daughter had conquered New York. She packed her suitcase and prepared to take the bus back to Mistra.

It gave her a start, seeing Jean alone in the car at the bus station.

"You're driving!" Gillie exclaimed. "Oh, of course, you've been sixteen for ages."

Jean said, "Gee, you look great! You're all glamoured up. When you first got off the bus I didn't even know you."

"I'm still me. And be careful. I'm valuable down in New York."

With a good-natured snort, Jean started the engine. Gillie looked intently at the town as they drove through it. Of course it wasn't changed, but it did look different—small, uninteresting, and a little shabby.

Dad greeted her outside with a reticent kiss, and Mom, in the warm, rich-smelling kitchen, hugged her as though she had been gone for years.

"Ward's coming to dinner tonight, to see you," Mom said. "We can't wait to hear all about the play and everything, but you'd better save it until we're all together."

Gillie went to her room. It had the air of a place long deserted. The bedspread was impeccably smooth, the writing table and bureau spotless and clear of the clutter of living. They had been keeping the room shut off to save heat, but it was warm now. She hung up her clothes and lay down on the bed, with only the light from the hall to keep her company.

At dinner they asked question after question. She managed to make her early experiences light and amusing. They loved the stories of Dulce, and they seemed to feel Gillie was truly grown up, having her own apartment. She told about her trip to Staten Island and her job with Mr. Deckter. She described the play until she grew tired of her own voice.

"Now let me eat," she laughed. "You talk for a while."

Long afterward, as she was on her way to bed, Jean followed her into her room. "Who's this guy Ralph? He must be sort of special, or didn't you mean it to show?" She sat down on the bed and doodled with a fringe of the spread.

"Oh—he's a good friend." Gillie was pleased at her own composure. "I do like him, but—you know. He's just a person who's fun to be with."

"I was curious, that's all. It sounded as if he might be kind of important. I thought it might mean you were getting over Jim."

"Oh, goodness, I've gotten 'way over Jim."

And I have, Gillie thought. Haven't I?

She remembered looking so carefully at the streets

of Mistra as they went past. Had she hoped to see him? Had she dreaded it, perhaps?

"Did you know they were expecting?"

"Who?"

"Jim and Betty, of course. It's supposed to come next May. Mr. Albert brags to anybody who goes in the hardware store. It's his first grandchild."

Gillie wondered if her smile looked as glazed as it felt. Jean soon left, and Gillie stood in the middle of the floor. It all came rushing back—the picture she used to have of her life with Jim. After it had ended, she had managed to paint for herself a new image, one of Betty's life with Jim. She saw Betty as a dull housewife with nothing to do but dust the cottage and weed the petunias. Or was it nasturtiums?

Now they would be a family. It was the first time she had thought of Betty and Jim as a family. Betty would have a place where she belonged, a safe place in a magic circle of love. They would be the happiest little family in the world. All while Gillie went back to the rat race, to the auditions, the rebuffs, the pavement-pounding, the temporary typing jobs.

With tears in her eyes, she gazed out at the apple trees, bare and cold in the November moonlight.

When it came time to leave, she was not sorry, though homesickness gripped her all over again at going away from her family. She looked forward to returning to New York, to the purposeful activity of finding new work, a new part to play. It was hard, but it gave her something Betty would not have in her serene, predictable life. It gave her the chance to struggle and to climb. She knew she would miss it if she stopped now. She knew she would hate herself always if she gave up after one bit part in a play that had flopped. If she could get that part, she could get others. Better ones.

She looked forward, too, to seeing her friends again—Dulce, Barney, Ralph, and all the others. There was nobody like them in Mistra.

It was late Sunday night when she unlocked the door, eager for the cheeriness of lamplight and Dulce.

The apartment was dark. She turned on a light and it seemed to increase the emptiness. She realized that Dulce must be spending the night at her home and would come in on a morning train. Gillie would not see her until Monday evening.

She closed the door. Now she would have to unpack and go to bed alone. The bleakness of the room brought back her fears and sorrows, and she wanted nothing more than to be home again where people loved her. Why had she thought it would be good to come back? Why had she wanted to plunge into it all over again? It was no fun at all to wonder that would happen next.

She dropped her coat over a chair and made a cup

of instant coffee. When her suitcase was emptied she undressed, put on her bathrobe and turned on the television to watch a late movie. In the morning she would phone Quick-Help and get another job.

Chapter Sixteen

In Mistra, where the cold was crisp and still, Gillie had loved winter. But in New York there was a constant driving wind that swept down the streets between the canyons of buildings, forcing the cold through her clothing and the soot into her face.

Yet the store windows were decorated for Christmas and soon there would be Santa Clauses and Salvation Army bands on every block. Dulce was full of excitement. Gillie wished she could share it. She climbed into bed on Sunday night with nothing to look forward to but getting up in the morning, making her sandwich for lunch, and taking a subway to the office. It was not even *her* office, as Mr. Deckter's had been. She was only a stranger sitting at a spare typing table against the wall.

Ralph . . . that was the trouble. She had looked forward to the Christmas season, to sharing it with Ralph. She had called him on her return from Mistra a week ago. He had said he would be seeing her in a day or two, but he had never called back.

She stared at the hump her toes made under the blankets.

I want to see him so badly, she thought. I just want to be with him. It can't be all over. We *liked* each other.

She reached up, snapped off the light, and stayed half sitting in her bed.

"Want to tell me?" asked Dulce. "I have the feeling you're not relaxed. Is something on the mind?"

"Oh, nothing serious. I just wish tonight would last a hundred years, like in *Brigadoon.*" She would not tell Dulce how much she longed for Ralph.

"You can't stand your job?"

"Could you? One more day of watching those idiotic office girls swaggering around, and I'll screech. And the ugly-looking thing who sits next to me and thinks he's so desirable . . . Dulce, your place isn't like that. These people are absolutely deadly, and my job is even worse. Or am I just prejudiced against office work?"

"That's what you get for being a drifter," Dulce said sleepily. "You should find a place and stick to it. Get to know the people and like them. I'll tell you if I hear of an opening at NATV." There was a crunch as she turned over in bed.

By Wednesday Gillie had lived more than two weeks without Ralph. Each day she had lost a little more hope of ever seeing him again.

She felt tears coming as she rode home on the

crowded subway. People were carrying packages. Everybody was happy. They all had places to go and people to love. She got off at Eighty-sixth Street and braced herself for the bitter winds that swept toward her from the river. At the newsstand she bought a New York *Times* and, on impulse, a copy of *Performers Only*.

That night it was another makeshift supper. She could not be bothered planning meals for herself, and Dulce was out on a date. Gillie sat on the couch to eat with *Performers Only* spread out beside her. The muffled sound of Christmas carols from a radio next door came through the wall. Her cheese sandwich was dry in her mouth and the reheated leftovers were sickening. She turned the pages of her paper, burying herself in the crackling world of show business.

A name caught her eye.

"Cornell Avedon!" she exclaimed. "I know him!"

It was a small item, one paragraph long. This time, instead of writing a play, he had bought one, a comedy. Plans indefinite as yet . . .

Clutching the paper for all the strength it could give her, she picked up the phone and dialed Mr. Avedon's number.

"It's Gillie Polk, your schizophrenic," she told him brightly. "I hear you're starting a new production."

His voice was dry and businesslike. "That's still up in the air. I'm afraid I can't tell you anything yet."

"Yes, I know. That's what the paper said. But I

thought if it became definite, I'd like a chance to read. If there are any parts I could do." Her self-assurance was wavering. "Are you going to be holding readings?"

"We have most of it cast now. That is, pending a firming up of production plans. There are a few bit parts vacant. I'll let you know."

"Oh, would you, Corny? Thanks an awful lot. I hope I didn't interrupt your dinner."

She sat curled on the couch, mulling over the conversation. He had been discouraging, but he had not said flatly "no." That alone would keep her from giving up.

A few days later she telephoned him again. He was still vague about his plans. She waited two more days and called him a third time. He told her to come for a reading on Friday and gave her the address of a studio he had rented.

It was happening again. Another audition. This time she had to be brave and go through with it. At least it was a comedy. She had enjoyed playing comedy at college, and had been good at it.

She found an empty chair in the studio and looked about at the others who had come to read. She had thought she might feel something of an insider, having known the producer before. But he was not even there. It made no difference anyway. She was as frightened as ever and as lost as she had been in the very beginning.

Win That Game! was a frothy story of a college football intrigue, set in the early part of the century. The major parts were cast and all it needed were a few more boys and girls. First, with one of the boys, she read an eight-line comic love scene.

The director smiled. He was a round and happy man named Gus, very different from Mr. Wales. He thanked her and told her to sit tight and not run away.

Others read. Gus thanked them all, and some he did not ask to stay. Gillie waited, philosophically calm. She remembered Dulce's offer to help her find a job at NATV. It made a safe harbor in which to anchor her hopes in case she did not get a part in this play. It was easy to get into an office.

She watched the other players, those who already had their parts. There was the lead—a sweet girl whose knack for romance was the basis of the plot. But more fun yet was the part of Josie, the second girl lead. She was lively, athletic, and attractive. It was she who planned the intrigue around which the play was written.

The girl who played Josie was beautiful and a natural comedienne. Gillie watched her enviously.

If I had her looks and talent, she thought, I'd have been a smash hit long ago. I'd a thousand times rather be an actress like her than Marsha.

"You over there by the window," she heard.

People were looking at her. Gus had called her forward. She rose, was handed a script, and found herself reading the part of a girl gone wild with cheering at the game.

She jumped up and down, waved her arms, and cheered as she had not cheered since high school. As the script directed, she turned to hug the man standing in back of her, only to realize that he was the college president.

She ended the scene, amazed. She was enjoying herself—had even forgotten she was reading for a part.

Gus's smile was broader than ever. Again he thanked her and told her to sit tight. Other girls played the same scene and then she was called again.

"Think you can do that in a long skirt?" Gus asked when she had finished.

The stage manager checked her name and phone number. She stayed until the audition was over. When she went home it was late in the evening.

"What happened?" Dulce exclaimed. "You look as if you'd eloped or something."

She and Barney were sitting on the floor watching television, with a gallon jug of cider and a box of jelly doughnuts beside them. Gillie's stomach turned. She discovered she was hungry.

"Dulce—" She opened the refrigerator to take out the makings of a sandwich. "Don't you know there are other things in this world besides romance?"

"Possibly," said Dulce, "but they don't count for much. Have some cider and doughnuts. Now tell me, what did happen?"

"I don't know. I really don't know."

126

And she didn't. She had not the remotest idea whether or not the part was hers. It only sounded as though it might be. But she had discovered one thing for certain. If she was meant to be an actress at all, she was meant for comedy.

Later she learned that Dulce and Barney had been planning a Christmas party.

"We're giving it jointly," Dulce said. "It's going to be here because our place is nicer. Is that okay?"

"Fine," said Gillie. Trying to speak casually, she asked, "Do you think Ralph will be coming?"

"Most likely, I guess. Why? Is that good or bad?"

"It's . . . it's good. Why shouldn't he come?"

"Well, I didn't know how you felt about him."

Gillie shrugged. She did not want to talk about it with Dulce, who always had such success with boys and who never seemed to care about any one of them in particular. Dulce would not understand her problem.

If Ralph did not come, Gillie decided, it would mean he definitely did not want to see her. On the other hand, if he did come, it would mean either that he did want to see her, or that he did not even care enough about their relationship to stay away.

Dulce and Gillie bought a tree two feet tall, set it on an end table, and trimmed it together. It was a silly thing, but it was Christmas—her first away from her family. She would spend Christmas day itself

127

with Dulce and her parents. Though she was a little afraid of Dulce's mother, it was better than being alone.

Already she missed the familiar cosiness and cheer of home. Last year she had been with Jim and he had given her the ring, her diamond engagement ring. They had had dinner with her family and then gone to his. Many of her presents had been house-keeping things.

Thinking of home and Jim made her feel lonelier than ever. She missed the love and security she had had then. But she realized she did not really miss Jim himself. She even hated him a little, for what he had done to her.

Gillie stood back to admire the tree. They had lighted it with a string of miniature bulbs, which were reflected in the red and gold ornaments.

"Artistic, I must say," Dulce commented.

"It's lovely," Gillie told her. "Just lovely, Dulce." She gazed at the lights until she was almost hypno-tized.

I wish Ralph could see it, she thought. I think he'd like it.

Saturday was the day of the party. Gillie was too busy all morning to think much about Ralph, until the phone rang.

"It's *him*," mouthed Dulce, gesticulating toward the receiver.

"Hi," said Ralph.

The friendly sound of his voice almost made her want to cry with relief. She had missed him so much. But, at the same time, she did not know what to answer. Why had he called? To tell her that he could come to the party, or that he could not?

"How have you been?" Gillie asked.

"Okay, I guess. Tearing around like some kind of nut. Wait till I tell you what I've been up to."

"What *have* you been up to?" she asked, glad that he could not see the eagerness on her face.

"I've turned to crime."

"You what?"

"I mean I've found a great way to make a living. I got this TV mobster part and they've been dragging us all over town to shoot the scenes. That's why I didn't get to call you. Not only that, I auditioned for a Broadway show, but didn't make it. I flunked a screen test, too."

"Oh, Ralph."

"Oh Ralph, what? I know it sounds crazy, but I'm glad about the test. It would have meant going out to the Coast, and I didn't want to leave New York. Not for a long time. I want to stay here and see a whole lot more of you, starting tonight."

"You're coming tonight? That's terrific!" said Gillie, trying not to sound too excited. "Why don't you come early and help us?" she added. "It would be good for you, after all that loafing."

Chapter Seventeen

"Dear Jean," Gillie wrote. "So glad you can come to visit in spring vacation. You'll be the first to use our sofa-bed. I'm pretty sure *Win That Game!* will still be running. It opened with terrific reviews and it's been packed every performance. My part's short but loud. At least you'll see me. I'm on stage a lot, and the stage is small. In fact, the whole theater only seats 172 people. The audience is on three sides of us. I never played like that before and it made me nervous at first, being right out in their laps, but I'm getting used to it. You feel as if they're in it with you, instead of just watching.

"Oh, yes, you asked about Ralph. Did I tell you he got on TV? I've been seeing a lot of him, but I'm still not sure where we stand. He came to my opening night, of course, but he brought an old girlfriend of his, a noisy thing named Marsha. They came backstage to see me and, boy, did I die. Naturally I didn't show it. Well, I don't want to get serious anyway. I'm concentrating on my career."

Jean wrote back: "I can hardly wait to see you in the play! And don't worry about your part being small. I'll bring a microscope. You can tell Ralph for me that I think he's stupid to bother with the noisy thing when he could have you."

Could he? wondered Gillie. I don't even want to think about it. It'll be a cold day in July before I go out on a limb and hurt myself again.

It seemed now as though she had never quite known where she was headed before. With *Win That Game!* everything had fallen into place. She knew herself as an actress.

She investigated acting classes, but they were still beyond her means. Instead, she learned what she could from library books. In a little while, perhaps, she would have saved enough to join a workshop. Then she would be one of the charmed circle. With that training, there was no telling where she might go.

Ralph came to see the play again, and this time he did not bring Marsha. Afterward he took Gillie home. They sat in the living room drinking hot chocolate and speaking softly, so as not to wake Dulce.

"You know, you were right," said Ralph. "You're a natural for comedy. I knew you shouldn't have been discouraged by *The Shores*."

"Thanks. I wish I could play this kind of thing all

my life. What about you, Ralph? You must be feeling pretty good yourself, now that you've made TV."

"Well, it helps. I think I have a lead on another part."

"Really? That's great!"

"I don't know, it's the same kind of thing. I'd hate to be stuck with that. You know—typed."

"But at least you're getting somewhere."

"Yes, but where? It's awfully hard to break out of a type. Do you think I'm so tough-looking? That's all they'll even consider me for on TV. Toughs. I want variety."

"You're not tough-looking at all," she said softly. "Not to me."

He had been resting his elbow on the back of the couch. Now he straightened his arm and slipped it around her shoulders.

"You're an angel," he whispered.

Gillie kept her eyes fixed on the rug as she snuggled in his arms. She reached up, took his hand and pressed it to her cheek. Her eyes closed blissfully. What a delicious, floating feeling! If only it could go on forever.

She did not know how long they sat together, neither saying a word. At last Ralph straightened up, pulling away from her.

"Someday," he said, "do you know what I want to do?"

"No, what?"

"I've been thinking about it for a long time. I'd like

to start a little theater, maybe a repertory company, someplace where they don't have any. Don't you think it's stupid that everybody has to come to New York or Hollywood to act? We should have provincial theaters all over the country, the way England does. Then you wouldn't have all these actors doing nothing. There would be jobs for everybody."

"It's a terrific idea," said Gillie. "But how would you start it? Anyway, I bet most people would rather be in a big city. I love New York. *I* wouldn't want to go anywhere else."

"Not even if you knew you'd be acting, and that if you stayed in New York you probably wouldn't be? I don't know how I'll start my theater, but I'm going to, someday. Gee, Gillie, with that set-up you could be acting all the time. You could play all the parts you wanted, and give plays you really liked. Isn't that much better than this crazy, hit-or-miss way we do it here?"

"I don't know," said Gillie. "I never really thought about it. I just like New York."

She had played her cheering scene for more than a month, and now it was early March. The play was still the popular success it had started out. To Gillie's surprise, even her short and energetic part remained fresh to her. At each performance it was as though she were doing it for the first time.

She continued to watch Anne, the girl who played Josie, whom she had admired even at the audition.

From her she might learn how an actress could be funny and lovely at the same time. A comedienne did not need to be grotesque, and Anne proved it.

Entering the dressing room before a Wednesday matinee, Gillie was shocked to hear that Anne was leaving.

"How come?" she asked in astonishment. "Did you find something better?"

"I think so," said Anne. "It's a smaller part than this, but it's a national company."

"A road show? The road show of a Broadway play?"

"Yep. It's prestige. And think of the experience, being with name actors."

"Won't you get tired of traveling?"

"I'll tell you after I've tried it a while. It sounds fun, though, and I'll see the country with all my expenses paid."

Maybe it will happen to me someday, Gillie thought. That . . . and maybe the next step is Broadway itself.

It was odd to think back and remember that she had once expected to land on Broadway immediately. Now she knew it was the pinnacle of a long, hard climb that might last for years. Even if you did reach Broadway, it was no guarantee you were there to stay. Several of the people in this very cast had Broadway shows to their credit.

She sat at her dressing table long after the matinee, when everyone else had left. It was snowing outside.

When would spring come? But snow in Greenwich Village was pretty, and not bleak, as it might have been elsewhere.

She was glad that this production was in a Village theater instead of on the Lower East Side again. It was a funny little theater. The dressing rooms were under the stage, and there was no way to get up during the performance except through a trap door onto the street. After that, it was a dash of only a few feet to the theater entrance—but long enough for passers-by to do a double-take at seeing Edwardian costumes emerging from a hole in the sidewalk. Sometimes the cast would find strangers descending the steps into the dressing rooms. Some of them mistook it for a subway entrance. Others wanted to find out where the pretty girls were coming from.

She opened her compact to put on street make-up for going home. There was a knock on the dressing room door.

"Come in," she called.

It was Gus. "My lucky day!" he greeted her. "Just the girl I wanted to see. I didn't think anybody'd still be here."

Gillie set down the lipstick she was about to put on and waited to hear what had gone wrong with her performance.

"You know Anne's leaving," said Gus.

She nodded.

"Understudy's leaving, too," he went on. "She's

getting married. How would you like to read for the part?"

Gillie stared. The room was spinning. What had he said?

"How about right now?" he suggested.

He expected her to answer.

"Okay." Her voice was a hoarse croak. She rose and followed him up to the stage.

Josie Hornblower? One of the leads? Did he really mean Gillie? Maybe she was only to understudy, but even that . . .

Gus gave her a sampling of scenes to read, while he played all the other parts. She could not believe she was really speaking those lines—Anne's lines. Josie was poised, popular, and dazzlingly funny.

It's not me at all, thought Gillie. But this is the way I want to be, and I can do it!

At nearly every entrance, Josie would appear with a hockey stick or a tennis racket. Gillie was thankful. It kept her hands busy. She was frightened of making mistakes, but she was happy, because Josie was happy. It gave her the energy and champagne brilliance Josie needed.

In some ways it was easier than a cold audition, for she was familiar with the play and the role. In other ways it was much harder. The standard had been set by Anne. She had to keep reminding herself that her own Josie would be different. She must do it her way and not Anne's.

I'm not playing a part, she told herself. I'm just

having fun. Having fun . . . Nothing to panic about. I'm having fun. This is only a game I'm playing. It doesn't matter. Nothing's at stake. It's fun, that's all. It's fun . . .

"Well, let's give it a try," said Gus at last.

She collapsed into one of the front-row seats, grateful for the dimness of the theater even when the house lights were on. She felt glassy-eyed and tired.

"We'll start rehearsing you tomorrow," he said. "We'll see how you do, but I think it's going to work out. Then," he added, half talking to himself, "we've got to find a chick to replace you."

To replace *me?* she thought. Some little hopeful is going to replace me, and I'm going to be one of the stars! Oh, what's happening? The whole world is upside down.

She wished there were not another performance that evening. It was too much to expect from her. She wanted Ralph. She wanted Dulce. Anybody. She had to talk to someone, for right now nothing seemed real.

Chapter Eighteen

A horse-drawn flower wagon rested at the curb. Its
sunny daffodils, narcissus, and purple and red anem-
ones were a mass of brilliance in the white sunshine
of early spring.

"Oh, Ralph!" Gillie cried. "Isn't it beautiful? Don't
you love it?"

"Which kind do you like?" he asked.

"All of them!"

He bought her a bouquet of daffodils. She held
them against her face. "Thanks, Ralph, that was
sweet. They're one of my favorite flowers."

With their clasped hands swinging between them,
they walked on down Fifth Avenue to sit in Washington Square park.

"I think I like the Village best of anywhere right
now," she said. "This is how I imagine Paris in the
springtime."

The park was dotted with couples like themselves. Many of them were college students from
New York University. Old men sat on benches feed-
ing the pigeons, or played chess at tables around the
edge of the park. Mothers were out with their baby

carriages. For a moment, Gillie thought of Betty. Her child would be coming in two months. Gillie wondered what it would look like. It would probably be a boy. She could not imagine Betty with anyone but a boy.

She looked at Ralph and found him looking at her. He leaned toward her as though to kiss her, but then he backed away. There were too many people around.

Gillie murmured: "Ralph."

"What is it?"

"Nothing."

I love him, she thought. I really love him.

A bubble of joy rose up through her and she wanted to laugh out loud. She closed her eyes to stifle it, then opened them again, her cheeks flushed. She hoped it would stay this way—a lighthearted, planless love.

"How come you're looking so gorgeous?" Ralph asked.

"I guess spring agrees with me," Gillie answered, smiling. She looked down at the daffodils. "And you do, too."

"Who, me or the flowers?" He took her hand. "All I can say is, I sure am glad that screen test didn't work out."

"You'll probably have other chances. And it's spring all the time in Los Angeles, I hear."

"It wasn't the weather I was talking about." He ran a finger through her hair.

"Would you want to try again? Or are you aiming more for Broadway?"

His boyishness disappeared. "I wish I knew. All I know is, I don't feel I'm getting anywhere now. More than anything, I want to be a good actor, and I'm not one yet. I don't feel anything solid under me. I just pitch in, try to get inside the character and play the scene the best way I know how, but I'm never really sure of myself. At this rate it's all going to bust pretty soon. I'm not growing."

"You studied for a while, didn't you? And you said it helped. Why don't we join an actors' workshop together?"

He nodded. "Maybe a summer course."

"Oh, Ralph . . ." She leaned back her head to feel the sun on her face. "I know I should worry about my career, too. I should think of where I'm going and how I'm going to get there, but right now I can't get upset about anything. I'm too happy."

"You're balmy. You've got spring fever." He pulled her to her feet. "This is the right kind of day to be balmy. No more worrying about where anybody's going."

Still holding hands, they walked on through the park.

It was hard to realize that in three months she would have been in New York a whole year. And look, she thought, at where I am!

It was all believable—except for getting the part of

Josie Hornblower. She still could not quite understand it. Gus must have known, from the way she handled her smaller role, that she could play Josie. He was an experienced director and so of course he knew what he was doing. But still, after her luckless months of making the rounds, after her disappointment in her first play, *this*? She looked into the mirror as she dressed to meet Jean at the terminal.

I guess I do have what it takes, she decided. That's lucky, because nothing could have stopped me anyway.

"Gil-leee!" Jean flung herself from the bus and hugged her sister. "Oh, Gillie, isn't it stupendous that I could come? Have you started your new part yet?"

"A week ago."

"Were you scared?"

"Of course. I always am. But it's a happy kind of scared. The bigger the part the more scared I am, and the more excited I am, too. Jean, I love it so much I'd die if I couldn't act."

They took a bus up Broadway and Gillie pointed out the sights.

"This," said Jean, "is a city! This is where I'm going to live. Just being here makes you want to do things."

"I know," Gillie replied. "Nothing could get me away from here. This place is *me* now. I almost felt like a foreigner when I went back to Mistra at Thanksgiving."

They visited the United Nations, the Empire State Building, and Radio City, where they lunched with Dulce. Jean went twice to see *Win That Game!* They wandered through stores and bought hats for the Easter church service. They helped Dulce decorate eggs for their Sunday dinner with Ralph and his roommates.

All week the weather was prematurely sultry and the sun hot. On Monday, Gillie took her sister to the Central Park Zoo. They had bought sandwiches at a delicatessen, and ate sitting on a park bench, finishing their meal with ice cream bought from a pushcart vendor.

"This is the life, Gillie," said Jean. "You've got it made. Aren't you glad that Jim—well, that things worked out the way they did?"

That evening, as Ralph still had some money from his television appearance and Gillie had the night off, he took them both to dinner at an Italian restaurant in the Village.

Jean was delighted. "It's the first Italian food I've ever had, except spaghetti dinners you buy in a package, grated cheese and all."

"Or ravioli out of a can," added Gillie. "And pizza. But they always seem native U.S., somehow."

Jean turned to Ralph. "I caught your TV show. You were marvelous. I mean it. I think you've got a great future as a hood."

"You and the casting people," he said. "Only they

never called it 'great.' I bet you expected a crook when you met me."

"Oh, no. Not after what Gillie told us about you."

He looked at Gillie. She pretended to be fascinated by her fork.

"I guess it would be dull if that was all you did," Jean agreed.

"That's all they seem to think I can do," said Ralph. "I've got to get out of it soon or I'm dead as an actor."

"Got any plans?"

"I'm not sure yet."

The waiter handed them a menu for dessert. Gillie said, "I think you should stick with it until you really get known. And while you're at it, you can find me a part on TV, too. I'd make a terrific police-woman."

"He's an awfully nice guy," said Jean as Gillie waited with her for the bus to begin loading.

"I think so, too."

"That's pretty obvious. But what are you doing about it?"

"Don't you think some things are better left alone?"

"Why?" asked Jean. "If you don't grab him, some-body else will. And he's an actor, same as you. You could marry him and it wouldn't botch up your career."

"Well, he hasn't asked me, so I don't have to worry about it. Besides, it's nice the way it is. We see each other all the time, but nobody's trying to make anything out of it that might lead to trouble."

"You mean you're not even thinking about marriage or anything?"

"Not for a long, long time," said Gillie.

The crowd began to surge forward and they said good-by. Afterward, Gillie wandered through the terminal by herself, gazing idly into the shop windows.

She loved Ralph. Jean had seen it. She loved him, and it wasn't only the spring air gone to her head. He seemed to love her, too. She had not meant it to happen. She had meant only to act and be a success. She should have had other boyfriends, as Dulce did, and then perhaps she would not have grown so fond of him.

But she was not Dulce, she was Gillie, and it was Gillie's life she was living. She and Ralph would simply go on the way they were. They were having fun. They both had their work and they had each other. Why not enjoy the present and let the future bring what it may? In the meantime, life was lovely and fun and she was successful, and that, after all, was really why she had come to New York.

Chapter Nineteen

The applause went on and on. Another performance was over. She would never grow tired of the sound of applause and never take it for granted. Beyond the stage lights she could see the audience, as during the curtain call she turned to all three sides for her first real look at them.

Quickly, before the illusion could be destroyed, the actors vanished from the stage, down the steps to the dressing room, and became themselves again. Above their heads the audience shuffled out across the wooden floor.

Later, she emerged from the theater onto the street. Lifting her face into the soft night, she was met by a full moon above the Village skyline.

It's perfect, Gillie thought. My life right now is perfect.

She caught sight of Ralph.

"Hi!" she exclaimed. "Don't you know stage-door Johnnies are out of fashion?"

He smiled as though he had not even heard her. They linked arms and walked aimlessly down the street.

"It's so nice and warm," she said after a while. "Is it always this warm in spring?"

"Sometimes. You never know. Sometimes it snows in April, too."

"In late April?"

"No, not this late."

He seemed to be only partly with her. She wished he could stop brooding on his career. She wished that somehow he could start on just the path he wanted, as she had.

They stood outside an espresso shop that was filled with an after-theater crowd.

"How about some coffee?" he suggested.

He led her to a small round table and they sat in ice-cream parlor chairs. Gillie had never been in this café before. It had an odd, decadent elegance. The menu offered every imaginable type of coffee, and she ordered iced cappuccino—espresso with whipped cream and cinnamon.

The walls were hung with original paintings, the work of Village artists. Her eyes wandered over the other patrons. It was the first time she had been in an espresso shop with normal-looking people instead of unshaven characters in dirty jeans.

Ralph had gulped down his coffee and ordered another. He was making conversation, but not seriously. Whatever was on his mind, he was not saying it.

"Finished?" he asked as she set down her glass. "Let's walk some more."

On and on they went until finally they stopped at a bench on the edge of Washington Square park. The moon was shining through the trees. How lovely it was!

Ralph sat turned so that he was facing her. "I think I've found something that might be my answer."

"That's wonderful! What is it?"

He took a crumpled letter out of his pocket. "I figured I wouldn't say anything until I got a definite answer from them. I wanted something concrete to tell you."

"Well, come on, what's the mystery?"

He grinned uneasily. "You ever heard of Franconia College?"

She shook her head.

"It's in New Hampshire. A girls' school."

"A *girls'* school!"

He stopped her before she could exclaim further. "That's the whole point. It's an all-girl college with a first-class drama department. They do top plays, classical and experimental, and they've got a brilliant faculty. The only thing they don't have is actors for the male parts, so they hire them. Guys like me, who've done professional work. It's an opportunity, Gillie," he argued emphatically. "I'll get all the training and experience I want, both acting and directing.

147

I'll have my chance to develop and grow, instead of just beating my head on a wall."

"Do you really want to do that?" she asked incredulously.

"That's what I want. There's no glory in it. Not even as much as there is in playing a TV hood. But at least I'll get a chance to become an actor."

"You're an actor now!"

"Gillie, do you realize all the groundwork that goes into acting? I think that's what's the matter with me. I haven't had the groundwork. I started right in acting and so far I've had some luck, but it was only luck. I've no solid training. And luck doesn't last forever. That's why I feel as if I'm at a dead end already, because I can't grow any more with nothing to grow on."

"But you can study in New York."

He was firm. "Not when I can do this. I want to get away from New York. Away from all the pressures."

It's happened, she thought. He's leaving me.

As she looked ahead to the next year, her panic rose. In spite of her beautiful part in a hit play, the joy was gone out of the future. Everything was dead. She wished she had never known him.

"You said you didn't want to go away."

"I didn't want to," he said. "I didn't want to leave you. That was the only reason. But this is different, Gillie. I want you to go with me."

He took her hand and held it tightly. She caught her breath. Every thought in her head shattered into bits of colored glass. This was Ralph, sitting beside her. Ralph—asking her to be his wife.

Hours later it still made no sense. She did not even attempt to go to bed. She sat in the living room with a glass of buttermilk, trying to look at her situation rationally.

"You'd have all the privileges of a faculty wife," Ralph had told her. "We'd get our room and board and a little spending money. You could take some courses, too. You could study drama there, and act. It would be good training for you as well as me."

In the light from a street lamp his eyes had burned with eagerness as he tried to make it sound appealing. She had said nothing. If she had opened her mouth she would have cried, for she loved him so much and could not bear to hurt him.

But the play . . . She had crashed off-Broadway and was close to being a star. She was so very, very lucky. Now the man she loved was asking her to give it all up, almost as soon as it had begun.

She woke in the morning to find Dulce standing before the sofa, staring at her.

"I fell asleep," Gillie said blankly.

"Are you sick?" Dulce bent down to touch her forehead.

Gillie had not meant to tell her. It wasn't fair to Ralph to go about telling people, and she did not want others interfering. But it was all so wonderful, so frightening and confusing that it burst out uninvited.

"Ralph wants me to marry him."

Instantly, because Dulce was about to let loose a stream of skyrockets, she explained.

"It isn't that easy. He's leaving town. He's going away to some college in New Hampshire and he wants me to go there, too. To bury myself in a little New England girls' school when I've got off-Broadway by the tail. Oh, Dulce, it isn't fair to make a girl decide such things, and please, please don't tell me what you think I should do, because you're all for marriage every time. But don't you see? What I'm doing is important to me, too. Everything's important. Everything." She fell back limply into a corner of the sofa.

"How long is he going to be there?" Dulce asked.

"A year. Maybe two years."

"Well, then, can't you be engaged? And when he comes back—"

"He's not coming back. He means to go someplace where they don't have any theater, and start one of his own. Dulce, I love New York. It's exciting and glamorous and . . . and it's home. I want to be here, where everything *is*. I want to go on doing what I'm doing now because nothing else would matter to me after this. Maybe Ralph and I aren't meant for each other, if he wants to give it up, and it means my life to me."

150

"Do you love him?"

"Oh, I do, Dulce, I really do. But I'm not ready to think about marriage yet for a long time. And now I have to decide in just a little while. Do you think maybe I don't love him enough if there's any doubt in my mind?"

"I'm sure you do," said Dulce. "It's not Ralph you're in doubt about. And it wouldn't be fair to him if you rushed off now and then blamed him later when you started missing off-Broadway. Me, I wouldn't have that trouble, because there's nothing I especially care about except guys, but I sort of know how you feel."

"I can't put it into words," said Gillie. "But it does something to me, being here. I grew up in a small town and I liked it then. I always thought a city couldn't have a heart. But it does. A great, big, *live* heart. And the theater . . . this is where things happen."

"I suppose it wouldn't be safe to let him go up there alone anyway," said Dulce. "He'd be sort of on the rebound, if he thought you didn't care enough about him to make up your mind. And he is attractive. And all those girls . . ."

"I guess it's now or never. But if I marry him, it means giving up everything else I love."

For a while they both remained silent. Then, as though she had an answer, Dulce jumped up.

"I'll make you some coffee," she said decisively.

During the day Gillie managed to sleep a little, and at seven-thirty she went to the theater to sit paralyzed in front of her make-up mirror.

An abundance of riches, she thought. I've such an abundance of riches that I don't know which to choose, and I'm as miserable as if I didn't have a thing.

How soon would she have to decide? It was almost the end of April. College opened late in September and they could be married around Labor Day. But of course Ralph would want to know sooner. He had a right.

"Hey, there, Polk." Fingers snapped in front of her face. "Want me to go on for you?"

It was her understudy.

With slow, unthinking motions, Gillie tied back her hair and reached for the cold cream. What would happen if she did marry him? There she would be, stuck in that little faculty apartment at Franconia College. She would begin thinking of all she had won and had given up, and she would be miserable. Winter would come and it would snow and she would remember the snowy day when Gus had called her up to the stage to read for Josie. How could she bear it?

Even if she did join the college drama department, so what? It would not be the same. It would not be professional. She would be able to take courses and work toward a Bachelor of Arts degree, which she did not need in the slightest. Ralph had told her all she would have there, and it sounded like a big, hollow nothing. The only thing she would have that she really wanted was Ralph. She wanted him so badly her heart was aching. If she could bear all the rest, he would be hers, for always. But could she? That would be for always, too. She could never come back to this.

She remembered that day in the park when he had bought the daffodils and it had seemed as though spring would last forever. She remembered their first date, the trip to Staten Island. She remembered all the funny little coffee houses they had visited together, and the time they had toasted marshmallows over candle flames. And the many, many times they had simply talked. Was all that over now? She would be alone again next year. As alone as she had been after Betty got the ring.

Gillie looked around the dressing room. Leave all this behind? She daubed on her greasepaint, pausing to breathe its delicious, stagy smell. She could hear the early ones arriving in the audience, and she closed her eyes, remembering the applause.

She was a professional actress in New York City. She had come to New York to act, and she had succeeded. This was only the beginning. There was still Broadway. She had not even had a chance at Broadway yet. How could she give it all up? How could she possibly leave everything she had, and everything she dreamed of—knowing she was never to come back?

If only—she wished it now with all her heart—if only she had not been given this big, wonderful break. She might have been able to leave the smaller part. If only Anne had not left the cast, or Gus had picked someone else to play Josie. If only . . .

Chapter Twenty

It was time to leave the train. Gillie suddenly wished she did not have to leave, that she could go on with Ralph. But she had had her chance.

"Good-by, Ralph. Good luck."

"Take care of yourself," he said.

She walked back along the platform and up the ramp toward the concourse of Grand Central Terminal. It was her fault he was going away. He would not have taken a summer theater job if she had told him "yes." He would have stayed in the city with her until the fall, and then they would have been married. Would have been . . . but she had chosen her career instead.

It was Saturday and there was a matinee that day. For the first time her spirit was gone. Her performance, she knew, was flat.

What if I never see him again? she thought as she stood on the make-believe bleachers watching a make-believe game. She had always believed in it before. Today she saw nothing but curtained walls and the glaring beam from a spotlight.

I'll get over it. I'll have to get over it. I can't go on being torn to pieces like this. I got over Jim, but I had to. With Ralph it's harder. I'm the one who let him go.

She wondered if he would write to her. She would not have been surprised if he didn't. He might want to forget her as she had wanted to forget Jim.

The weather grew hot. Sultry summer air crept in to lie heavily on the city.

"I wish we were air-conditioned," Dulce said one morning. "Do you think Mother would ever relent on my living expenses and buy us an air conditioner? If it gets too bad, I may have to take a bed roll and sleep in my office."

"At least you have a cool place to work," Gillie told her. "Our theater's murder. The building's too old to air condition, and we're already losing audience. It's even worse for us actors because we've got the stage lights on us."

She had noticed, as everyone had, that the audience was dwindling. Surely it was the weather, and soon the heat spell would have to break.

All winter and spring the play had been such a success that she was not prepared for the closing notice the cast found posted one night.

Closing! Throughout the performance she could think of nothing else. They were closing in two weeks.

After the show Gillie dressed quickly and left the theater alone. She started to walk toward the subway. There was the coffee shop where she had been with Ralph the night he asked her to marry him. She crossed the street, went inside, and sat down at one of the tables.

A foursome of bit players from her own cast drifted in and took a table behind her. She sipped her cappuccino, pretending not to see them. Two more weeks and Josie Hornblower would be only a memory. What did one do after the closing of a show? One started all over again. She knew that much. She would order another batch of pictures and begin making the rounds just as though nothing had happened. It would be exactly like last summer.

No, not exactly. Something had happened which would be very important from now on. She had played a lead in an off-Broadway production.

She finished her coffee and left, glancing toward the bit players on her way out. How lucky she was. How very much luckier than they.

She was back on the creaking elevator that took her up to Mr. Borisov's studios. How much she had to tell him! Now he would be dealing with a professional, and not just another hopeful.

She had three pictures taken in her Josie costumes and five in contemporary dress. On leaving the studio, she bought a copy of *Performers Only*. She turned to the casting page. The calls, as usual, were for chorus dancers and more chorus dancers. There was nothing on television that week, but she would try again when she had her composites.

By the time her pictures were ready, a new issue of *Performers Only* was on the newsstands. She studied it carefully. Still there was nothing in television, nothing but commercials. They did not want actresses for commercials, they wanted models, with models' faces.

After spending a morning wondering what to do, she stopped at Radio City for lunch with Dulce.

Gillie felt irritated. She was discouraged and hungry. "I'm going overboard," she said to Dulce. "I'm having two hamburgers, French fries and cole slaw and—"

"Are you trying to get a job in a circus?"

"Dulce, what's the matter with television? How can they have so many shows and not need any actors?"

"Honey, don't you know where all the shows are filmed? If you want to get on television, you'd better start heading for California."

"But Ralph got into two that were made in New York."

"Yes, there are a couple of crime serials. But you have to look like a cop or a crook or a gangster's girl. That's why Ralph was so lucky. They thought he was a crook."

The waitress set down her hamburgers and Gillie piled them high with relish.

"Do you think I could pass for a gangster's girl?"

"No."

"A murder victim, maybe?"

"Gil, dear," Dulce said. "You should have married Ralph."

At Dulce's suggestion she went again to the NATV casting office. She had expected it to be different this time, but she might as well have never been a star. After her reading she was thanked, and a copy of her new composite was accepted for the files. They would forget about her just as they had the first time.

Wearily each day she made the rounds. By evening her feet were tired, almost too tired to carry her on stage. Hardly anyone was casting, and nobody cared about Josie. They were no more interested in her than they had been the year before.

On the day before the play was to close, Gillie telephoned Gus.

"I'll be going hungry pretty soon," she told him. "I can't even get an audition. There's nothing on TV unless I go out to California, and I haven't the money. Do you know of *anybody* who's casting? I'll be glad to take a walk-on. Anything."

"There isn't much doing in summer, you know," said Gus. "Unless some summer stock company wants a replacement."

"Do any?"

"None that I know of."

"But I need a job."

"Of course there's always office work or department stores," he suggested. "Can you type? Try one of those temporary office job agencies. A lot of actors tide themselves over that way."

"But Gus, I want to act! I can't stop now. I was

just beginning to get somewhere. Why is it so hard to find work even after a part like mine?"

"I know," said Gus. "It's rotten, but that's show business."

Nothing. Nothing. Gillie sat by the telephone, glaring at it. Why did show business have to be so rotten? There was no other field like it. People clamored for secretaries, teachers, and nurses, but nobody had a job for an actress.

She spent her first free night watching television.

"Hey," said Dulce. "I could fix you up with somebody."

"I don't want to be fixed up with anybody. I want Ralph."

"Too bad his theater doesn't need actresses. Hey, maybe they do! Why don't you write them? Wouldn't that be funny? You could show up there without telling him and—"

"I don't want to go there," said Gillie. "I want him to be here."

"Oh. Well, too bad."

Gillie wondered why, since Dulce was so thoroughly in favor of marriage, she did not get married herself and mind her own business.

"I'm going for a walk," she said. "It might be cooler outside."

The night air was soothing and soft and the sky more luminous than ever in the high humidity. Gillie walked aimlessly eastward. Along the way, ground-floor tenants had left their shades up to receive the breeze, casually sharing their lives with passers-by.

I *love* this city, she told herself passionately. She stood on the corner of Broadway and Eighty-sixth Street.

I'll never leave it. Never.

It seemed odd not to be taking the subway down to Greenwich Village. She wandered toward the entrance, hearing the roar of a train below her. Removing a token from her purse, she hesitated, then descended the stairs.

Now what am I doing this for? she wondered as she stood on the platform.

The train came. She took her place among the passengers and rode until she reached the Village.

She walked on and on, through bright and lively streets. These had been their streets, hers and Ralph's. There was a hollowness about them now— a loneliness, a sadness.

She turned a corner. There, coming toward her, was Hovis Kane.

"Hovis!" Gillie exclaimed. "Golly, it's funny, bumping into someone you know."

"Yeah?" said Hovis. "What's doing? Your show still running?"

"No, it just closed. What are you doing?"

"Collecting unemployment."

"How come you didn't go to summer stock?"

"Well, I thought I was all set with something

161

here," he said. "How'd I know it wouldn't keep going?"

They were standing on a corner. He asked her which way she was headed and she told him nowhere. They began walking.

"What sort of job did you have?" Gillie asked.

"I was doing a sketch in a night spot."

"Doing a what?"

"A comedy sketch. We ad libbed every night, depending on what was happening in the news. Then they changed the show and we were out."

"So now you're making the rounds again."

"*I* don't know." He sounded discouraged.

"Are you giving it up?"

They had reached Washington Square park. This was where Ralph had proposed to her. An ache ran through her. She did not want to walk through the park, not with anyone but Ralph.

They sat down on a bench. Gillie looked about her. That evening with Ralph came back so clearly that for a moment it was more real than the present.

"What are you doing down in the Village?" she asked.

"Just been returning a coat. I had somebody's heavy coat for the winter. Finally decided I didn't need it any more. Whew!" He tugged at the collar of his sports shirt.

"Did you say you're giving up acting?"

"I don't know. I'm thinking about it."

"What would you do?"

"Go back home, maybe. Get a job in a bank or something."

They gazed across the park into the night, talking but not looking at each other as they meditated on the puzzling world of show business.

"If a person could only get somewhere," Gillie said. "I mean, arrive. But you can't, it's not that easy. I thought I was there, but now I have to start all over again."

"Yeah, it's rough."

After they parted, Gillie sought out the bench where Ralph had proposed. No one was there. She sat on it alone, under the street light.

Hovis—living on unemployment checks. So poor he had to borrow a winter coat. No wonder he was planning to give up acting. If you succeeded, nothing could be more thrilling. But the chances of failure were a thousand times greater, and then—degradation.

She watched as people strolled through the park or along the street. She heard the sound of a guitar and saw a group of folk singers several benches away. The Village on a summer night! It was home even more than Mistra had ever been, perhaps because it was adopted. Mistra she had always taken for granted. She wondered if native New Yorkers felt the same blasé acceptance of their city as she did of Mistra. How could they? And how could anyone, *anyone,* ever leave it?

Ralph had liked it, too, and he had left. Did he

miss it now that he was away? And was his missing of it tangled up with his feeling for her? She wondered how he felt about her now. It had to be the same. He could never have loved her if he did not feel the pain that she was feeling at that moment. This night had made her long for him so terribly.

"Ralph, I love you," Gillie whispered. "I love you, I love you. I'll never find anybody else like you."

As she said it, Gillie knew that it was true. There was no one else in the world like Ralph, and Ralph was all that mattered. She could almost feel him sitting on the bench beside her as he had that April night. He had asked her to marry him, and she had not known what to do!

She rose and walked slowly along Washington Place. Down the winding streets in back of her was the theater where she had acted. It had been fun, playing Josie, but it was over now. All of a sudden she knew she did not want to go back to it. Even if she found another part just as good, she would not want it. Even if she became a star, even if she reached Broadway, what of it? What would any of it mean without Ralph?

She thought of Ralph, going off alone to do what he believed in. He had had to choose, too, between love and his work. But for him, the choice had been more obvious. What was there for him in New York? Gillie had been the selfish one. If Ralph had stayed with her, his career would have been at a dead end, and so he had had to leave. She wondered how he had felt, going away without her. Why hadn't he hated her for making him do it? But he hadn't.

Oh, Ralph, you're so wonderful, Gillie cried to herself. And I'm so stupid. I always wanted what *I* wanted, and I never thought of you or anyone else.

She felt as though a part of her had fallen away— the part that was a self-centered child. It was like a shell coming off, and she felt free. She had thought she was grown up when she had come to New York to act. She had thought that independence meant adulthood. But now she knew that the answer was not independence. It was sharing. It was wanting to build a life with someone else.

She hurried toward the subway, impatient to get home. She would write to him immediately and would mail the letter that night. Once, Ralph had thought she would bring him happiness. She prayed that he would still think so. She wanted him to be happy. She wanted their life together.

Chapter Twenty-One

"Gil, I'm proud of you," Dulce said as she helped Gillie out to a taxi. "I knew it would have to happen, but I was awfully scared it wouldn't."

"I was worried, too, for a while," Gillie replied. "I didn't want him to think it was just because of the play closing and me not being able to find another part. I probably could have found something, once the fall season opened. But you know, Dulce? I didn't even care any more. It's such an empty way to live, for me, at least. I know there are loads of people who thrive on it, but I guess I'm not one of them."

A taxi drew up and Gillie climbed in while Dulce piled the suitcases in after her.

"Heck," said Dulce. "I'll go with you to the station. Move over." She slid into an empty corner of the seat.

The morning was fuzzy and fair, the promise of another hot day, but the city's bustle went on as always. Her last day in New York was the same kind of day as her first, so that it was hard to believe she

166

was leaving. She recalled every sensation of that
other summer morning a year ago when she had
walked down Forty-fifth Street—the heat, the soot,
the steamy air, and her excitement at just being
there. She remembered, too, thinking that all she had
to do was decide to be an actress, and she would
surely find a part in a play.

I certainly learned a lot in a year, Gillie thought.
And I did succeed, even better than I had a right
to, considering how hard it is.

A redcap met them at the station and took her
bags. Dulce stayed with her while she bought her
ticket and a magazine. At the train gate they paused.

"It's not really good-by," said Gillie. "I'll be seeing you next month."

"In Mistra, of all places." Dulce was sniffling a
little. "Gee, Gil, what are you trying to do, make me
feel like an old maid?"

"Why? Because I'm getting married first? Honestly, Dulce, I thought you'd be 'way ahead of me."

Dulce broke into a giggle. "So did I."

"Anyhow, it won't be long. I'm tossing my bouquet straight to you."

"I always knew you were a pal. 'By, bride."

"'By, bridesmaid. And Dulce—I hope you find
somebody as—as really *nice* as Ralph. You deserve
the best there is."

They kissed each other and Gillie went on to the
train.

Minutes later she was passing among the tene-

ments of East Harlem. She saw dusty plants growing in pots on fire escapes, and bored faces, lean-
ing on arms, gazing endlessly out of the windows.

"Good-by to you, too, New York," Gillie murmured.

The train crossed the Harlem River, leaving Manhattan. Gillie looked at her watch. There were hours
more to go before she would see Ralph. Restlessly
she opened her magazine.

The city slipped by and she watched it but did
not see it. She was counting the hours. She was
imagining what it would be like to step off the train
and find Ralph waiting for her. He had said he could
cut a rehearsal to come and meet her. It was almost
six weeks since she had seen him. After her visit she
would go home to Mistra to help her mother plan
for the wedding.

Her wedding. In a month she would be married.

When she had received Ralph's answer to her letter, she had cried. He was so wonderful. It was
hard to believe that she had ever thought of giving
him up. How could anything have seemed more important than Ralph? Her time on the New York
stage had been fun and she would always remember it, as she remembered her senior prom or her
two years at college. But most of all, it had given
her experience. It had prepared her for her life with
Ralph and the theater they would create together.